PETALS OF PERIL

A LAKE MINNETONKA COZY MYSTERY

BOOK TWO

LYSSA LUND

Dedicated to all of my horrible online dates, which helped me to recognize when I'd found "the one"

CONTENTS

PROLOGUE

"*S*o, I guess you guys are official now."

Ignoring the small stab of envy that slammed through her heart when Veronica nodded, Sarah tried to smile.

"Yeah, we are." Veronica chuckled, picking up her glass of wine, her cheeks a little pink. "Who'd have guessed I'd have run into Chase so many years later?" She took a sip of her wine. "*And* that he'd still be such a nice guy."

This time, Sarah's sigh caught everyone's attention. Heat built in her face as she waved with one hand. "Don't mind me."

"Oh, but now we're *all* interested." Annie grinned. She tilted her head and swung one leg over the other as she sat back in her chair. "What's got you sighing so heavily?"

"Nothing." Sarah shrugged, but her three friends just looked back at her without saying a word. They'd been friends for a long time, and it didn't look like any of them would believe her. With a groan, she rolled her eyes and set her wine glass on the side table. "I'm happy for you, Veronica. Really, I am. I just wish..." Hesitating, she looked steadily at

Veronica, hoping her friend wouldn't be upset with her for being so honest. "I just wish I had some of your luck."

"I didn't get so lucky the first time," Veronica reminded her with a wry smile. "The divorce was hard."

A stab of guilt pushed its way into Sarah's heart. "Yeah, I remember. I'm sorry."

"Not saying I don't understand." Veronica waved a hand as the other two nodded. "I think we *all* get where you are."

"Except I don't need a man to make me happy," Deborah quipped, making them all laugh.

Sarah grinned. "I get that – and I don't think I need a man to be happy either. I guess I'd just like to meet someone who was actually genuine." Rolling her eyes, she shook her head. "Remember the last guy I dated after I used that dating app? It didn't exactly go well."

"But you shouldn't let that put you off." With a shrug, Annie took a sip of her mock-tail. "Plus, that was a long time ago, wasn't it?" Wincing, Sarah let out a laugh. "Don't remind me. It's been *ages*."

Deborah giggled, and soon, the room filled with laughter. Giving herself a slight shake, Sarah shifted to sit back in her chair a little further. She could always be honest with her friends, and she appreciated that. Deborah was right. She didn't *need* a man to make her happy. She had a lot of happiness in her life already, but seeing Veronica and Chase had made that desire begin to grow again. "I don't know. Maybe I should try dating again."

Her last date had been a complete and utter disaster. Yes, it had been months ago, but still, that memory wouldn't leave her alone.

"Hı!" Her nerves were like butterflies already. So far, Anthony seemed like a great guy, and she had to hope his profile picture was genuine. They'd messaged via the dating app for the last few days before he'd asked her to meet, and ever since she'd said yes, her nerves had been growing. Meeting someone was different from just sending the occasional message.

It's going to be fine, Sarah.

Anthony sounded really good on paper. He'd told her he had a steady job, he lived in the small town next to hers, and that he was looking to start something serious, *if* they hit it off, that was. So she'd agreed to meet him for dinner.

Just gotta pray it goes well.

"Hi there, can I help you?" The girl behind the counter smiled, making Sarah realize she hadn't said anything for a while. "Oh, I'm sorry. Yes, I'm here to meet someone for dinner." Embarrassment caught her throat. *She doesn't need to know it's a blind date.* "Sorry, what I should say is I have a reservation. It's under 'Hayes'."

The girl smiled, nodded, and then looked at her screen for a second. "Oh yes, I see it. Your friend hasn't arrived yet."

"That's okay." Aware she was a few minutes early, Sarah glanced behind her, just in case her date had come in while she was standing at the desk.

No luck.

"Can I order a glass of white wine, please?"

The smile that lifted the girl's mouth made Sarah blush. Okay, she was nervous. *Really* nervous, but maybe she was making that a little too obvious.

"Sure, no problem, I'll have that right over to you straight away. If you would just follow me."

Following the server, Sarah was soon seated at a corner table. The light music quickly eased her nerves, and the wine – which had come immediately definitely helped. The minutes ticked by, and, taking another sip, she took her cell out and set it on the table.

What if he calls to say he can't make it? What if he walks into the restaurant, sees me, and walks right out again?

When ten minutes came and went, Sarah shifted in her seat. She was hot, clammy, and uncomfortable, wondering if everyone in the restaurant was looking at her, wondering why she was sitting by herself. *Maybe I can pretend it's just a modern thing. I'm sure plenty of people come out to eat by themselves.*

Her eyes went to her wine glass.

Except I'm not eating

Swallowing, she licked her lips, thinking perhaps she should just order. He was already almost fifteen minutes late. Maybe he was going to turn out to be a jerk after all.

"Sarah?"

Her mouth was full of wine. She turned, spluttering, then grabbed her napkin to dab at her mouth, her face hot.

"Oh, hi, Anthony." Her eyes slowly took him in. He was tall, with fair hair and a wide smile, wearing jeans and a navy shirt. Her gaze quickly zeroed in on the logo on his shirt. Okay, so he was exactly like he looked in the picture... minus the pizza delivery company logo.

"Nice to meet you." Quickly, Anthony sat down. "I'm so sorry I'm late."

Sarah blinked, slowly withdrawing her hand, which she'd stretched out for him to shake. Something felt...off. "Did you come straight from work?" Silently kicking herself for never asking him what his job was, she forced a smile, stretching it wide.

"Yeah, sort of." Anthony grinned, flashing her a white-toothed smile, his brown eyes warm. His hair was slicked back, but not so much by gel. Sarah wondered if he'd been wearing a baseball cap, which he'd only just remembered to take off. There was a small imprint of a band around his forehead.

I'm not going to judge an appearance.

"I can see you've already started." Lifting one hand, he clicked his fingers in the air, catching the attention of one of the servers. "I'll get a beer, please. Just the one. Thanks." With a grin, he looked at her. "Have you ordered yet?"

"No." Taking a breath, she let her smile fix in place. *At least I'm not being stood up.* "Would you like to order? Here's the menu. I know what I would like."

"I know I would like, too." His smile spread even wider, something flashing in his eyes, but Sarah looked away and didn't return it.

He said he wanted something serious. I'm not here for a one-night stand.

"Pizza?" Before she could stop herself, the suggestion sprang into the air between them, her eyes going to the logo on his shirt again. "Is this what you do for a living?"

"Yeah, I do." His grin turned into laughter as he leaned across the table. "I never get a chance to eat it, though, so maybe that suggestion is a good one!"

Sarah's smile dropped. "Right."

This wasn't what she'd been expecting. Her expectation for the evening hadn't been to sit across from a guy who would drink beer and eat pizza. Grimacing, she looked away from him, only for shame to fall hard on her head. Who was she to judge an appearance? After all, she was the one who had suggested pizza in the first place. They'd hit it off so far over messaging. Perhaps she needed to give it a little more time.

They ordered quickly – he the pizza and she the risotto, and Sarah tried to smile and tried to push away her nagging feelings of doubt.

Anthony took a swig of his beer. "So what do you do?"

"I'm an attorney." Wishing they'd exchanged job details beforehand so she hadn't been so surprised when she'd learned he delivered pizza, Sarah shrugged. "It's a demanding job, but I love it."

"So, what sort of stuff do you do in your attorney job?" His eyes twinkled. "I wonder if you've had to represent any of my friends?"

Her words stuck in her throat, not quite sure if he was joking or not. Thankfully, she didn't have to answer since their food arrived, and all of Anthony's attention went straight to his pizza.

"This looks good, huh?" He picked up a slice without hesitating, only for something to stop him.

His cell phone.

The ringing seemed to echo through the whole restaurant, and Sarah's stomach began to churn. "Sorry. Do you want to get that?" Trying to keep her smile fixed, it waned a little when he shook his head.

"Na, it's okay."

He let it ring, and Sarah cringed at every single chime. She didn't mind if she had his cell phone with him - she had hers too – but surely the least he could do was to silence his notifications for a while. And he definitely didn't need to leave it sitting out on the table like that.

"So, like I was saying –"

For the second time, Anthony picked up a slice of pizza, and again, his cell rang loudly. The jangle clashed with the gentle music around the restaurant, and Sarah winced visibly as a couple nearby turned to stare.

"Sorry." Sighing, he ended the call. "I'm meant to be on my break. I guess they forgot that."

What? Sarah blinked, trying to take in what she'd just heard. "You mean you're working tonight?"

Anthony nodded, biting off a bit of pizza and chewing it furiously. "Yeah, but like I said, I'm on my break." Shrugging, he smiled at her before swallowing the pizza and washing it down with a glug of beer. "That's why I can only have one beer tonight, though. I've only got about an hour."

A slow flush began to climb up her chest, spreading heat up into her neck. "You mean to say you're not planning on spending the evening with me?"

Without even a pause, Anthony shrugged both shoulders. "It's our first date so I didn't think I'd need to."

The heat continued to rise to her face. Was that really how much she meant to him already? The fact that he could only give her an hour of his time — and on an evening when he was working? Hadn't he had any other time free?

"Like I said, it's a steady job." Grinning as if she'd understand, Anthony reached for his beer again. "But from the sounds of it seems like your job is way better than mine. Better paid too, I bet."

"I guess." Talking about her salary wasn't exactly something she had planned to do tonight, but then again, she'd never imagined that a pizza delivery guy would be spending his break with her in a restaurant.

"Maybe you can get the bill tonight, then?" Laughing, Anthony reached across the table and touched his fingers to hers. "Sound good?"

Not for the first time, Sarah was left speechless. Anthony laughed a little more, only to be interrupted by his cell phone ringing again, which was now for the third time.

Exasperated beyond belief, Sarah gestured to it, a tightness about her mouth. "I think you should get that."

Anthony didn't even seem to notice her frustration. Wiping his mouth with the back of his hand, he picked it up and answered the call. "Hello?"

Sarah took another sip of her wine.

"No, I'm on my break, and I'm with someone." He grinned in her direction, but Sarah only took another sip. "What do you mean, overtime?"

Anthony wasn't looking at her anymore. Instead, his eyes were on his pizza, as if wondering whether he could eat as much as he could before his break was up. "But I'm eating right now. And —" His words stopped abruptly. After another few seconds, he sighed, then chuckled. "Okay, okay, you've convinced me. I'll be there in ten."

Surely, he can't be thinking of leaving!

A chill ran through her, embarrassment opening up a gaping hole beneath her, pulling her down towards the floor.

"Looks like we're going to have to reschedule." With no apology in either his voice or in his words, Anthony smiled and then shrugged before looking away. "Let me just...." Snapping his fingers, he caught one of the server's attention as Sarah groaned, closing her eyes tight. "Do you think I can get this to go?"

This would have shocked her if Sarah hadn't been surprised enough already. Instead, she simply turned her head as the server took the pizza away, ready to put it into a box for Anthony.

"I hope you don't mind." Reaching out again, he squeezed her hand, and she tried not to flinch, even though that was her immediate reaction.

"Of course not." *What else was there to say?*

"I'll be in touch. We can do this again sometime. Properly. I mean."

Sarah caught his hand before he pulled away. "No, Anthony." She watched with interest as his eyebrows flew up towards his hairline.

"No?"

"As in, *no*, we won't be doing this again, properly or otherwise." She gave him a small smile. "I don't think we're a good match." Letting go of his hand, she lifted an eyebrow as Anthony scratched his head.

"Oh." Taking a beat, he smiled, shrugged, and then

grabbed the pizza from the server when he brought it over. "Fair enough. I hope you enjoy your risotto. It was nice to meet you."

Sarah held up her empty glass to the server as Anthony walked away. "Would it be possible to get another glass of wine, please?"

The server nodded, smiling back at her. "Sure. And let's put this one on the house, shall we?"

Touched, Sarah managed a nod and a smile before looking back at her risotto. A sense of overwhelming loneliness took hold, and she sucked in air, trying to push it back. Her hopes had been dashed the second Anthony had walked into the restaurant in his work uniform, and he stomped all over her dreams when he'd told her he was on his break. Now, he had decided that overtime was more important than getting to know her.

I sure can pick 'em.

Picking up her fork, she sighed. The very least she could do was salvage her risotto, and she intended to eat it with gusto after all that. Picking up a forkful, a sudden realization hit her, and she froze, her fork halfway to her mouth.

And not only that, he's left me with the bill.

"SARAH, ARE YOU OKAY?"

Pulling herself back into the conversation, Sarah nodded at Veronica. "I'm fine. I was just thinking."

"About?"

With a dry laugh, she rolled her eyes. "About my last date."

"The pizza guy?" Deborah laughed and shook her head. "You gave up dating after that bad date?"

"Something like that." A streak of embarrassment ran through her. "I had one before that, too, remember? The guy didn't show up. Both of those together really put me off trying the dating scene, especially via any app."

"You just met one – or two bad apples," Veronica said firmly. "If you want to meet someone special, if you really want to make a go of things with someone, then you've got to get back out there. Don't let that bad experience put you off."

Nodding slowly, Sarah picked up her wine again. "I'll think about it."

"Great!" As all three chimed in together, Veronica, Deborah, and Annie shared a look and a smile. Narrowing her eyes, uncertain what they were doing, Sarah looked from one to the other. They were concocting something, she was sure.

"I said I'll *think* about it," she emphasized as all her friends giggled. "That doesn't mean I'm ready to open up that dating app again and start swiping."

Deborah was the one to answer. "What does being ready look like? Either you want to go out on a date, or you don't. From the way you sighed hearing about Veronica and Chase, I'm guessing you're *more* than ready."

A flutter of excitement wriggled in her stomach. "Maybe." Chuckling, she pulled out her cell and waggled it. "I guess that means I'd have to update my profile on that dating app."

"Or we could do it for you."

Before Sarah could say no, Deborah grabbed the cell out of her hand. With a shriek of protest, Sarah jumped out of her chair to retrieve it, but Veronica and Annie quickly ran over to protect Deborah.

"Come on, at least let us have a look at it for you?" Veronica's eyes were sparkling with laughter. "We know you the best, don't we? We'll be able to get you back on your feet and dating again in no time."

Annie squeezed Sarah's hand. "We promise."

SARAH

ne week later
"What are you guys doing?" Sarah narrowed her eyes as her three friends lifted their heads and stared at her, their faces frozen in innocence as Annie slowly put one hand behind her back. Only a few minutes ago, Sarah had gone to the kitchen to fix a few snacks and had returned to find the three of them clustered together in the living room.

"Nothing."

Sarah waggled a finger in Deborah's direction. "I can tell you're all lying to me, so you don't even *try* to pretend. What are you guys up to?" Tilting her head, she folded her arms across her chest, but her three friends said, "Come on."

It had been a week since her discussion with them about how she'd thought about dating again, and since then, Veronica, Deborah, and Annie hadn't stopped asking her about it. Every time she saw one of them, there had been some mention of it. Deborah had even gone as far as to suggest her cousin as someone Sarah could go out to dinner with, but Sarah had ended that conversation quickly. It was always a bad idea to date a friend's family. There was always the chance things could end badly, with the possibility of losing a friend in the aftermath.

"Well, one of you is going to tell me what you're doing, one way or the other." Hefting her chin, Sarah looked from one friend to the next. "So, come on. Confess!"

All three exchanged a glance, and after another few seconds, Deborah shrugged. "We just thought you might want to try a *new* dating app." Reluctantly, Annie pulled out her hand from behind her back and held out Sarah's cell phone. Stepping closer, Sarah put one hand to her heart, her breath hitching.

"Is that... me?" Aghast, her voice was a thin whisper. "Did you set up a profile for me on this?"

"Yes, we did." Veronica didn't hold back, speaking with as much honesty as usual. "You told us you were thinking about dating again. We just figured you might need a little push in the right direction – and this new app is meant to do great things!"

"This is more than just a little push." Sarah reached for the cell, but Annie withdrew it quickly. "This is a shove!"

"Yes, but look how great a catch you are!" Annie gestured to the screen, still holding it back from her. "*And* we just set you up a few minutes ago, and you've already got a match!"

Indignant flames ignited Sarah's heart, but as Annie grinned at her, they began to flicker and ebb away. "Really?"

Her cell dinged, and Deborah chuckled. "Make that two matches!"

Despite her frustration, Sarah's heart skipped a beat, and, without warning, she took back her cell phone from Annie's hand. "Let me see."

A shiver ran over her skin as she skimmed her profile. She had to admit that her friends had chosen a good photo, but she didn't have time to read everything they'd said about her. Scrolling back to the top, she clicked her 'matches' icon and looked at the first guy and then at the next. "I can't believe I've got two matches already."

"Why? What did you expect?" Deborah smiled and came to stand beside her. "So the first guy is Phillip? He says he's a farmer. And who's the other?"

Sarah clicked on his profile, and Deborah leaned into her, grinning.

"Now, *this* guy is really cute." Her head craned over Sarah's screen. "Look, he works in construction."

"Explains the muscles." Veronica nudged her, laughing as Sarah's face warmed. "What's his name?"

"Steve." Sarah studied the photograph. Steve was square-jawed but with kind blue eyes. He wasn't smiling in his profile picture, but that didn't turn her off. She thought it made him look a little mysterious.

"So what are you going to do." Annie wiggled her eyebrows. "Fancy going on a date with either of them?"

Taking a deep breath, Sarah looked down at the screen again. She ought to be annoyed with her friends for doing this, but the truth was, she was a little glad they'd done it, especially now that she had gotten two matches almost immediately. "I'm not sure."

"What is there to be sure about?" Veronica smiled when Sarah couldn't come up with an answer. "I get that it's scary setting foot back in the dating pool when you haven't done it for a while, but trust me, there's nothing to worry about. All you're doing is going out to dinner or for a drink - and if it doesn't work out with either of them, all you gotta do is go back to the app and look for someone new! You said it yourself, Sarah, you wanted to be with someone. You *want* to find someone special. This is a way of doing that."

Annie smiled quietly as Sarah managed a nod. "I don't think I would ever use a dating app personally, but I think this might work for you." Her head tipped. "What have you got to lose?"

It was a question Sarah couldn't answer. Just looking at Steve, she let her thoughts go back to Anthony, the pizza delivery guy who had ruined her expectations of dating – and to the guy before that who hadn't even shown up.

"Okay."

A smile bloomed on her face, and her three friends cheered and then wrapped their arms around her.

"This is so exciting." Veronica squeezed hard, laughed, and then stepped back. "You *have* to tell us how it goes."

"I will." Already sensing her doubts rising steadily like a floodwater, Sarah turned to Veronica, a sudden hope draining her doubts away. "How would you feel about a double date?"

Veronica's eyebrows shot towards her hairline. "You mean with me and Chase? When you go out with either Steve or Philip?"

She nodded. "Yes, if that would work. I'll definitely feel less nervous that way."

"Then, of course." Veronica smiled warmly. "Try not to worry. I'm sure these two dates are going to go great. Anthony was just a one-time thing."

"I guess." With a smile, she lifted both shoulders. "At least, I have to hope so.

This is bringing me serious déjà vu vibes.

Sarah had no idea why she'd picked the same restaurant as when she'd been out with Anthony, but when Phillip messaged her, asking her where she wanted to go for their date, she'd panicked and picked the same place she'd been with Danny. Even the music seemed familiar.

"Hi, I've got a reservation." Her eyes narrowed slightly.

Surely that couldn't be the same girl who had stood behind the counter all those months ago?

"What's the name?"

"Hayes." Sarah lifted her chin, determined not to make any mistakes tonight. She doesn't need anyone here to know she was out on a date... and a *blind* date at that.

"Of course. Right this way."

As they walked, the server looked over her shoulder. "Your friend is here already."

"Great."

Except I don't feel great.

When Phillip had arranged a date for dinner, it was the one night Chase couldn't attend, so she'd had to come alone. Sarah was flooded with nerves, worried Philip would turn out to be someone completely different from what he'd said on his profile. That was the worst thing about dating apps; people could pretend they were someone else.

"And here you are."

The server pulled back the chair for Sarah to sit in, but she didn't move, her feet fastened to the floor. The man who had gotten out of his chair to greet her was definitely *not* the guy she'd expected. This man was about ten years older than her, with thinning grey hair and glasses and without the athletic build he'd posted in his photos.

Oh no.

"Phillip?" Sarah ventured as the server melted away. "You *are* Phillip, right?"

Grinning, he stuck out one hand. "Yes, that's me," he confirmed as Sarah's fears began screaming at her, telling her that her friends had known this would happen.

"You don't look like your profile picture." Not wanting to make a scene by standing in the middle of the restaurant, she placed herself delicately on the edge of her chair.

The man shrugged. "Does it matter?" Still smiling, he sat

back down, turning himself to face her. "When I first saw your profile, I *knew* we were going to match. You're perfect for me."

Swallowing, she shook her head. "I don't really like being lied to."

To her frustration, he only laughed. "I didn't lie to you. I just used an old photo, that's all. The only important thing about a person is their character, right?"

Sarah searched his face. His smile was genuine, and she was sure he believed every word – and on the whole, she did too, but then again, she wouldn't have matched with him if she'd known he was so much older than she was. "Do you mind if I ask how old you are?"

Phillip shrugged. "No problem. I'm in my mid-fifties." Chuckling, he leaned across the table towards her, winking broadly. "But I won't be more specific than that."

Surprised, Sarah blinked. She definitely didn't have a problem with someone being a little older, but she wouldn't have matched with someone so much older. After all, she had only just hit forty. The fact he'd lied to her was pushing her away from him. First of all, he'd deliberately used an older photo of himself to appear younger than he actually was. And second, he'd never once warned her about that. It had been a deliberate deception.

"Come on." Phillip reached out one hand as if he could see her frustration, but Sarah didn't offer him hers. "You can't be annoyed with me about that. I'm sure not everything you said in your profile is true."

"Actually, it is." Sarah lifted her chin, glad her friends had decided to be completely honest about everything they'd put in her profile. "I'm exactly who I say I am. My profile picture is from last month."

Phillip's smile faded. "You're not going to hold this against me, are you?" He lifted his shoulders high and held his hands out. "I think you'd be great for me. I'm looking to get together with someone quite quickly, to be honest. A whole lot of work needs to be done at the farm."

The farm?

Blinking, Sarah waved the server away when she came close. There wouldn't be any need for a drink or even a meal right now. "I'm sorry, Phillip. The farm?"

"Yeah, that's what I said." Phillip grinned at her as if she should already know exactly what he meant. "That part of the profile was true, at least."

When he laughed, Sarah didn't join in.

"I mentioned I had a farm, I'm sure," he continued with a smile. "It's a lot of work for one person. My kids all help out, and the oldest one will probably take over in the next couple of years, but he'll need all the help he can get. Once he starts running the place, I'll be looking to retire, but I'd want us to stay close to the farm. Of course, we could stay here in Excelsior or think about living elsewhere. If he *takes over the farm like I hope,* he'd still need us around. An extra pair of hands here and there, you know? And to get plenty of advice from his old man." Chuckling softly, he lifted a shoulder again. "The farm belongs to the family. We'd have to make sure we did all we could to help it thrive for the next generation."

The way he said *we* made something tighten in her chest. She tried to laugh it off—but the feeling lingered, heavy and inexplicable. A cold hand gripped Sarah's heart. Somehow, Phillip had gone seamlessly from talking about himself to talking about the two of them together, as if they'd already stepped into a long-term relationship. In his mind, from this moment on, she would be tied to this man and his farm, helping him to settle down into retirement.

Yeah, I don't think so.

"Can I get you anything?"

Phillip looked up quickly. "Oh, I'll have whatever you're having, Sarah."

"I'm not having anything." Sarah managed a brief, apologetic smile. "I'm sorry. Would you mind giving us a few minutes?"

When she looked back at Phillip, his eyebrows had lifted, and his eyes were a little rounded. "What do you mean you're not having anything? My kids won't be here for another ninety minutes."

Sarah dragged in air. "I'm sorry?"

"They won't be here for another ninety minutes," he repeated as if it was perfectly normal for his children to be attending his date. "They really wanted to meet you. I showed them your profile, and after I talked to them about how great it would be for our family, they were all really excited."

This is a disaster.

Struggling to accept all of Phillip's explanations, Sarah took a breath. Why had she ever let her friends talk her into this? "You're going to have to tell them it didn't work out, Philip." Sarah got to her feet, speaking as calmly and firmly as possible. "I'm sorry."

"You can't leave." Phillip grabbed her hand in one quick movement, and she hastily turned back to face him, embarrassed to make a scene in front of the other tables. "We haven't even had anything to eat yet. You don't know anything about me."

Lifting her gaze, Sarah steadily looked back at him, choosing not to say anything, and as the silence grew, Philip seemed to shrink just a little.

He let go of her hand.

She took a breath. "First of all, I know enough to realize that you're not the sort of man I want to be with. You aren't honest, and I value that trait very highly. You deliberately used an old photo for your profile and pretended to be much younger than you actually are. Secondly, I have no interest in farming *or* in retiring. And thirdly, I would never expect to meet any of your children until I was in a long-term relationship, and that definitely won't happen."

Phillip's shoulders dropped as if somehow she had broken his heart by telling him they wouldn't work out. The words, *I'm sorry* came to her lips, but she refused to let them fall. She had nothing to be sorry for.

"I really don't think you're being fair."

"And I really don't care what you think." Aware she was being a little harsh, Sarah grabbed her bag. "Goodnight, Phillip. Please don't message me again."

With a toss of her head, she strode to the door, pulled it open, and walked out of the restaurant. Instead of going home, she swung into the nearest bar, her spirits sinking low. Finding a stool, she perched on the edge, pulled out her cell, and waved one hand in the bartender's direction.

"Hi."

Sarah looked up at him, a heaviness gripping her as she sank onto her seat. The bartender was drying a glass, but one eyebrow was cocked in her direction. He had sharp, angular features with dark eyes that glinted with interest when he smiled at her. "What can I get you?"

With a shrug, she grimaced. "Whatever is going to help me forget about what just happened."

"You sure about that?" He grinned, but Sarah struggled to smile back. "You might pay the price for that tomorrow."

"At this point, I don't care."

"I see." His smile was a little softer than she'd anticipated, and she was sure there was a glint of sympathy in his eyes. "That bad, huh?"

"The worst." Cocking her eyebrow, she tried to smile, but it broke into pieces. "So what should I have?"

"Well, what's your usual?"

Tilting her head, she thought for a moment. "I'm usually a white wine or a rosé."

"I've got that here." Gesturing behind the bar, he grinned back at her. "So how about a couple of shots to take the edge off, and then you go for your usual? That way, you won't regret it in the morning."

Sarah smiled at him, the sharp pain of meeting Phillip finally fading. "I thought you guys were meant to try to get as much liquor down your customers as possible."

Laughing, he pulled out a shot glass and sat it in front of her. "I'm not most guys."

"I can see that." Picking up the shot, she slugged it back, then set it down again, fighting to catch her breath as heat enveloped her chest. "Another." The word shot out in a half-gasp, half-shout, and the bartender grinned but obliged.

"I'll go get you that wine." While his back was turned, she picked up the second shot and threw it back, feeling the tension began to ebb. Her shoulders dropped, and she wiggled them lightly, smiling appreciatively when he set down a rather large glass of rosé in front of her.

"It's pretty quiet in here tonight." The bartender gestured to the half-empty bar. "You've got my full attention if you want to tell me what's happening."

Sarah's tongue ran lightly over her lips. Was he just being friendly, or was it something more? "Are you sure you want to hear about the worst date ever?" She held up one hand, silencing him before he could say anything. "In fact, do you want to hear about the worst *two* dates of my life? In all honesty, it's quite a sad story."

To her surprise, he put out the hand over hers for just a second. "I'm good with sad stories." A wry smile lifted his mouth. "I've had a fair share of them myself."

"If you're sure." When he lifted his hands, heat ran

through her as if he'd left something hot behind. A smidge of interest had her curling her toes, and when he dropped his hip at the counter, his dark eyes fixed solely on her, electricity pushed itself through her veins as she smiled back at him.

Perhaps this evening would turn out better than she'd expected after all.

VERONICA

*V*eronica tilted her head. "What do you think?"

"What do I think about what?"

Rolling her eyes, she smiled. "I can't even pretend to be frustrated with you. Not when you're looking at me like that."

Chase grinned at her. "Why else do you think I haven't been able to concentrate on what you're saying? You look amazing, Veronica."

His compliment put a wide smile on her face. "Thanks. I figured I'd dress up to go out tonight." She tipped her head. "But that wasn't what I was asking you about."

Chase said nothing, his gaze still roving down her form. Stepping forward, she took his hand, and his eyes shot to hers. "Do you think you can concentrate for maybe thirty seconds?" She laughed when his fingers laced with hers, his smile growing steadily.

"As long as you keep smiling at me like that, I'll do what-ever you ask." The dark flicker in his eyes had her catching her breath, and when he leaned in to kiss her. She responded at once, only to pull back, realizing she was losing her train of thought.

"Chase. This is important."

With a grin, his eyes glinting, he ran one finger lightly down her cheek. "Hey, I wasn't the one who leaned in like that."

With an effort, she pulled herself away. "I was trying to ask if you'd be willing to go out on a double date."

In an instant, Chase's expression changed, his eyebrows lifting high. "You mean tonight?"

"No." Putting both hands on her hips, she shook her head. "Haven't you been listening at all? I was talking to you about Sarah."

"Sarah." When he dragged out her name, she laughed and rolled her eyes.

"You're doing this on purpose."

"Am I?" One hand reached out for her, but she evaded him, dodging just out of his reach. He grinned wickedly, and she giggled. After what they'd endured, they'd had nothing but fun these last few months. And after deciding to go steady, they were having more fun than ever.

"You know who Sarah is," she told him, waggling one finger in his direction. "She's one of my best friends, remember?"

He nodded, but she could tell he wasn't really paying attention. Not the way his eyes were wandering up and down her. She didn't know whether to be pleased or exasperated. "She's been having a hard time with dates recently, although truthfully, she hasn't been dating for a while." With a sigh, she spread out her hands. "Probably because her last couple of dates were disasters."

That caught his attention. "Disasters? How?"

"A disaster in terms of the fact that one guy didn't show up at all, and the next guy turned out to be a pizza deliverer."

23

Her shoulders lifted. "That wasn't the problem, though. He turned up in his uniform and ended up taking a call to go deliver pizza in the middle of their date."

Wide eyes met her. "Are you serious?"

"It's absolutely true."

Chase let out a low whistle. "I can see why she might be a little reluctant to start dating then." With a shrug, he smiled. "What is it that you're asking me?"

"She's recently gotten the dating app back again. She had two guys interested, and she asked me if we might come with her on a double date. I thought it was a good idea. It might help encourage her back into the dating scene."

"Oh, sure." Without a pause, Chase smiled. "That sounds great."

Satisfied, Veronica smiled back at him and let him pull her into his arms. "I'd do anything for any of my friends, even if it means we have to share our date."

Chase wrapped his arms tight around her waist. "That is going to be tough. I'm used to having you all to myself." His lips settled on hers for a second, and she sighed, aware that just the slightest touch of his lips had her melting.

"Do you think we'll be able to survive?"

"Well…" Chase let out a heavy breath. "It looks like I don't have a choice but to endure it. Although," he finished, his eyes twinkling, "maybe you can think of a way to make it up to me."

The dark swirls in his eye sent in a familiar tug of longing. "I'm sure I can think of something."

Chuckling, Chase lowered his head. "I'm going to hold you to that."

"I AM SO glad you could join us."

Veronica smiled and sat back down in her chair as Steve

joined them. The double date had been planned quickly enough, and this guy, Steve, hadn't needed to be encouraged at all. What had made it all the better was that Chase already knew him, having worked with Steve a few years ago.

I hope it goes well.

Veronica glanced at Sarah before pulling her gaze away, glad that her friend had decided she was going to give dating another go. She watched with interest as Steve's eyes flickered across the table towards Sarah.

"So you know Chase?" Veronica asked, smiling when he answered her question but was still busy looking across at Sarah. *That's got to be a good sign.*

"Yes. I used to work with Chase before he set up his own company and decided to forget all about me." Steve grinned, and even Sarah laughed before asking him something else.

So far, so good. From looking at her friend, Veronica could tell Sarah was incredibly nervous, given how she sat bolt upright and how her smile was so tentative. Hopefully, the nerves would disappear quickly, and she'd soon be able to settle down.

"What sort of business are you in?"

Veronica smiled across the table at Chase as the conversation between Sarah and Steve picked up. They shared a lot in common. They both had a passion for the outdoors, although they both claimed they didn't get out much. This was followed by the discovery that Steve had a cat, and Sarah *also* had a cat. As Veronica grinned at Chase, there was a long discussion over the cats: where they'd each adopted them from, the colors of the cats, the foods the cats ate, the behavior of the cats, and where the cats slept. Veronica had very little to say, given that she didn't have a cat, but she didn't care. It was nice to see Sarah smiling.

"Shall we order?"

When there was a brief pause, Chase interrupted the cat

conversation with a wave of the menu. "The server is going to come over fairly soon, and I don't know about you, but I'm getting hungry."

"Oh, sure." Steve took the menu but handed it to Sarah. "Why don't you choose? I'll have a look when you're done."

Sarah's smile grew even bigger, and Veronica reached across to squeeze Chase's hand. So far, he seemed perfect. After a few minutes, Steve and Sarah were locked in conversation again, leaving Veronica and Chase to chat together.

"They certainly seem to be hitting it off." Chase's hand found her knee under the table. "Seems like our double date was a good idea."

"Yes, it was. Although you're still going to have to make it up to me." His eyes lit up as he grinned, and Veronica giggled.

"You're incorrigible."

"No, I'm not," came the quick reply. "I'm just head over heels in love with you."

She smiled at that, her heart full of him. She'd been by herself for a long time, locked between a divorce and loneliness. But then Chase had come along unexpectedly, and despite all the difficulties that had chased them for a while — none of which had been their fault, they'd finally found a bit of happiness.

"Can I take your orders, please?"

Veronica looked down at the menu, having completely forgotten what she wanted, preoccupied by Chase's flirting.

"Oh…uh…can I —?"

"Sarah?" Standing at the end of their table, the server let his hand fall to his side rather than being poised with pen over paper. "Sarah, is that you?"

Veronica glanced at the server, then looked straight towards Sarah. Her friend was looking at the server and then away, her eyes wide.

"Oh my goodness, how long has it been?"

Sarah's smile edged up on one side. "Obviously a little too long," came the direct answer. "I'm so sorry, I don't remember."

It was direct, but then Sarah was always reasonably direct. She'd stopped short of saying she'd forgotten completely who this person was and instead had smiled apologetically and said that she couldn't remember his name. Direct but diplomatic. It was a little uncomfortable, and Veronica looked down at the table, showing an unbridled interest in the menu rather than paying any attention to the conversation between them.

"Wait. You don't remember me?" The man rubbed one hand across his chin. He had dark eyes and a flashing smile, which had now disappeared completely. Sandy curls bounced when he shook his head. "It's okay. I guess I should have expected it. It's been a long time."

"I'm so sorry." Sarah smiled tightly. "I'm sure if you remind me, I'll remember."

His shoulders lifted. "It's Danny. We met in college, remember?"

Veronica could tell that Sarah remembered immediately, given the way her eyes widened, and she began to nod fervently. "Oh yes, of course. Danny, I'm so sorry. College was a while ago, and so much has happened since then. I –"

"Yes, I can see that. You decided to move back here?" Danny interrupted with a slight sharpness to his tone. "I didn't think you'd ever come back to Excelsior."

"Neither did I." Sarah's smile was a little forced to Veronica's eye. "But I guess we both ended back here after all."

Veronica cleared their throat, hoping to cut the tension. "Would you mind if we ordered?" She smiled just as her stomach rumbled, right on cue. "I'm getting real hungry."

Immediately, Danny snapped to attention. "Yes, of course,

I'm sorry." With a shake of his head, he gestured to his notebook. "What would you like?"

The conversation was seemingly forgotten, they quickly ordered their meal, with Steve looking at Sarah as Danny went away. "Are you okay?"

Sarah let out a slightly broken laugh. "Sorry. That was weird. I didn't expect that, and I'm sorry for interrupting our conversation."

"You didn't." With a small smile, Veronica tilted her head toward Danny's retreating figure. "*He* did." Sensing that something was a little off, she frowned. "Are you sure you're okay?"

"Yes. I haven't seen him for a long time. I'm just really embarrassed I forgot his name."

"I don't think you need to be. He didn't seem upset." Steve smiled at her. "Anyway, let's forget about it, and you can tell me more about yourself."

Chase exchanged glances with Veronica, leaning forward over the table as Steve and Sarah chatted about cats. "Was it just me, or was that a little weird?" Something about the way Danny had looked at Sarah lingered with her, though she couldn't quite put her finger on why.

"I'm sure it's nothing. I was just a bit worried for Sarah. She seemed shocked."

"Yes, she did." Keeping his voice low, Chase reached for Veronica's hand, squeezing it. "But I'm sure you could find the truth if she needed you to."

Quickly, Veronica screwed up her face. "I could, but only if Sarah wants me to. If there's nothing to tell, we'll take it for what it looks like." She shrugged. "Two old college friends meeting, one forgetting the other's name."

Chase hesitated for a second, then shrugged. "You're right."

She grinned at him. "I love it when you say that."

He laughed. "Well, if it makes you light up like that, then maybe I'll say it more often." Laughter bubbled to the surface again. "I'm glad you asked me to do this. I'm enjoying it so far, albeit without Danny's awkward conversation."

Veronica smiled, glancing over to where Sarah was busy talking to Steve like nothing had happened. "Yeah, I think so too." Sliding a glance in their direction and then looking back at Chase, she wiggled her eyebrows. "Maybe Sarah won't have to start dating at all. Maybe she'll hit it off right away."

A burst of laughter from Sarah and Steve had Chase grinning. "Maybe you're right." He squeezed her hand again. "Let's hope that this is the beginning of something beautiful."

SARAH

I'm sure that wasn't there a minute ago.

Frowning, Sarah paused at the front door as she gazed down at a single flower sitting on the step in front of her. She'd already been out once this morning to check on her cat, who always needed to be encouraged to come back into the house for breakfast, and when she'd come out, that flower had definitely not been there. Now it was sitting right outside her front doorstep as if the wind had been blown it there.

Except there was no wind this morning.

She bent down to pick it up, absently twisting the stem between her fingers. As she straightened, a faint awareness prickled between her shoulders—as if someone had been watching her, even though the street was empty.

With a small shake of her head, she dismissed the thought and carried the tulip down the path, setting it on the fence beside her car. It was a warm, sunny day. The date with Steve had gone great, and she hoped he would give her a call back —that he'd want to meet again. The only awkward moment had been when Danny had turned up, and she hadn't remembered him.

As if he'd known she was thinking of him, her cell rang, and Steve's name popped up. With a smile, she answered it. "Hi, Steve.

"Hi." She could hear the smile in his voice. "How are you this morning?"

"I'm great, thanks." she beamed. "How are you?"

"I'll be great once you promise to go out to dinner with me again."

There wasn't even a second of hesitation. "Sure, I'd love that. When were you thinking?"

"When are you free?"

She laughed along with him. "Why don't you suggest a date, and I'll tell you if I'm available." She was acting a little coy and grinned when he laughed.

"Don't make me beg for it," he growled, making her smile. "How about tomorrow?"

A broad smile crossed her face. "I'd love that. Saturday it is." Propping herself up against her car, she smiled and waved at the mailman. "I gotta go. Tell me where and when, and I'll be there."

"You got it."

She slipped her cell back into her pocket and took her letters from Joe, the mailman.

"Thanks, Joe. How are you today?"

"All the better for seeing you."

Sarah laughed, the last of the strange tension draining away. Joe was one of those steady, familiar faces that made the neighborhood feel safe.

Joe was a forty-something, tall, wiry man with dark hair swept to one side and a bright smile almost always on his face. They'd gotten to know each other over the last few months.

He was always ready to stop and talk, and she enjoyed chatting with him. He always had some story about goings-on in the neighborhood. No doubt he had another one for today.

"Good, thanks. You got a smile on your face already this morning. Must be a good day."

Unable to keep the smile from her face, she shrugged. "I finally managed to get myself a second date."

His eyebrows lifted. "A hot date? Good for you. Anyone I know?"

She shook her head. "Don't think so. I have a dating app, but Chase knows him as well, which is great. We all went on a double date."

"That would be Veronica's Chase?" Joe nodded sagely. "Well, I hope it goes well whenever it is. Looks like he's already put a smile on your face."

Joe is always so kind.

"How about you? You've never told me about anyone special in your life."

With a laugh, Joe shrugged, his eyes twinkling. "That's because there *isn't* anyone special in my life besides my dog." Grinning, he revealed absolutely no disappointment over that statement. "Married to the job, me." With a wave, he carried on, heading down the road. "Have a great day, and I hope your date goes really well."

Her cheeks were going to hurt from smiling but she couldn't help it. Climbing into her car, Sarah pulled the door shut and headed into work.

IT'S GOT to be the lunch hour now, surely?

With a quiet groan, Sarah looked up at the clock. Only an hour to go until she could go find something to eat. Friday was her most difficult day. Not because she wasn't busy but because she always felt like it was halfway to the weekend, and her motivation just fled. Right now, it was all she could do to keep her eyes open.

"Sarah Hayes?"

Turning in her chair, she waved one hand at her open office door. "That's me."

"Great." A young man walked into her office, and her eyes flared wide at the sight of beautiful flowers in his arms.

"Are these for me?"

The guy shrugged, entirely unaffected by the fact he was delivering beautiful flowers to someone. "If your name is Sarah Hayes, then yeah." A brief smirk touched his mouth. "Sign here, please."

She quickly scribbled her name on the line and took the vase from him. The flowers were beautiful, and she leaned in, inhaling deeply.

Something about them stopped her short.

I recognize that scent.

She couldn't work out what it was. Looking down at the flowers curiously, it finally came to her.

I've seen these flowers before.

Her heart twisted a little, her breath catching in her chest. These were the same flowers as the one she'd seen on her step that morning. Surely that couldn't be a coincidence?

"Ohhh, and who are these from?

Her colleague, Jane, walked into her office, setting down her papers and coming over to smell the flowers.

Sarah handed them to her. "I don't know."

She looked for a card, but there wasn't any. Separating each stem to see if one had fallen between them, no note was attached.

"You've got a secret admirer," Jane giggled, elbowing her lightly. "That's so exciting."

Except I don't feel excited.

"Yeah, they're really nice." Sarah couldn't hide the note of tension in her voice, catching a slight frown flick across Jane's face. "I'm just not used to getting flowers, I guess!" With a small shake of her head, she took a breath. *I'm probably overreacting.*

"You sure?" Jane didn't sound convinced.

"It's just strange they didn't have a note with them." Glancing at the discarded packaging, she picked one bit up as if she might find something. "It's strange not to have a note."

"Well, you were on a date last night, weren't you?

Sarah threw a look of surprise at her colleague, only for Jane to laugh. "Why, did you think it was a secret? Everybody here in Excelsior knows everything that's going on *all* of the time.

"Let me guess. Someone saw me there and decided they were going to tell you?" Sarah laughed as Jane rolled her eyes.

"Okay, so my sister was there with her husband." Jane grinned. "So naturally, she told me she'd seen you there. Did you have a good time?" Her eyes went to the flowers. "Obviously you did."

"I had a great evening, yeah. And you're right, these are probably from Steve." *I'm making something out of nothing.*

Jane squeezed her shoulder gently. "Of course, they are."

"Although it's weird that he didn't add a note."

Shrugging, Jane went across the room to pick up an empty vase sitting on the windowsill – one that looked a little dusty to Sarah's eyes. "He probably did. Maybe the flower company just forgot to put it in, or it got lost somewhere." She walked in the door. "I'll go fill this up. And while I do that, why don't you give him a call and find out?"

"Thanks, Jane." Thinking this was probably a good idea, Sarah picked up her cell. Instead of calling him, she sent a message instead.

Had a great night last night. And if these flowers are from you, then thank you!

She didn't have to wait long for his reply.

Sounds like you beat me to it. I've got flowers on order, but they shouldn't have been delivered yet. Maybe they came early?

The question mark at the end of his message made her smile. Obviously, these flowers were from Steve. She'd just been letting her mind run wild, thinking about the flower she'd seen on her doorstep that morning. It had just been a coincidence.

"They're gorgeous. I love them. Thank you."

"Well?" Jane returned with her vase full of water, and smiling, Sarah walked across the room to set her flowers in the vase. "Are they from him?"

"Yes, they were." Sarah laughed when her friend chuckled. "And no need to say I told you so. You were right. The note must have just gotten lost somewhere."

Jane grinned. "I'm glad. These flowers are beautiful. I hope you're going out with him again?"

"I am." With a smile, Sarah sat back at her desk, admiring the blooms. "Thank you. Was there something you had for me?"

It took Jane a second to remember why she'd come into Sarah's office in the first place. "Oh yes, I needed you to look at these papers." Hurrying across to Sarah's desk, she picked up the stack of papers she'd set down, having been distracted by the flowers. "I was just going to ask you about –"

"Delivery!" Another knock at the door had Sarah twisting around in her chair while Jane turned at the same time.

"Another?" Jane's eyes flared wide. "Wow, he must really like you!"

Sarah's heart, which had only just begun to quiet down, suddenly leaped into another furious rhythm, a little panicked when another young man stepped into her office holding a big bunch of flowers. This bouquet contained roses, daisies, and even a sunflower, but not a single one like the tulip she'd found that morning.

"And here's the note with them."

Taking the flowers, she set them down carefully and, once the delivery man had stepped away, she ripped open the little envelope to get the card.

'I really enjoyed meeting you. Looking forward to going out with you again.'

It was signed by Steve, and as she read the card for a second time, Sarah's skin prickled with sudden uncertainty. If these were the flowers from Steve, then who had sent the tulips?

She almost reached for her phone to call Steve—then stopped. It felt too soon to explain something she didn't understand herself.

"Sarah?"

Sarah barely glanced at the man at her door. Her head was filled with questions and her stomach roiled. "Yes?"

"I have something for you. I just wanted to say how great it is to be working in your department and I...."

The rest of what he said turned into a loud buzzing as Sarah gazed at the tulips until the only sound she could hear was her heart pounding.

Just who had sent her the tulips, and why had they kept their identity secret?

THE QUESTION PLAYED on her mind all through the rest of the day. Even when she finished work and headed to her car, ready to go home, the question still sat there. Who had sent her those flowers? And why had they put one on her doorstep? Her heart beat hard as she pulled out her car keys, hating that she couldn't even *begin* to consider who might have sent them. Lifting her head, she made her way to the car only to stop dead, her eyes fixed on her windshield.

There it was. A single tulip, kept in place by one of the wipers on her windshield. Her mouth went dry as she pulled it out.

Who would have done this? And why?

An uncomfortable prickling ran down her spine, and she glanced around the parking lot, her heart in her throat. Someone had placed the tulip here. Someone had put it on her car windshield, securing it so it wouldn't blow away. They had *wanted* her to see it, had wanted her to come out at the end of the day and not miss it.

A sudden thought made her eyebrows raise.

"Of course." All of her fear melted away as, with a roll of her eyes, she dropped the tulip to the ground and climbed into her car. There was nothing to be worried about. This *had* to be the work of her friends.

The more she thought about it, the more sense it made. It had nothing to do with Steve or anyone else she'd dated. She had three very good friends, all of whom knew she had been a little on edge lately, who had talked to her about dating again, and who had all listened to her sigh about whether or not she would ever find love. Was this their way of making sure she was encouraged to keep going with her return to dating?

She smiled. "I bet they sent those flowers without a note, so I'd think they'd come from Steve." Murmuring aloud, she laughed softly.

Turns out they didn't need to after all.

Pulling up her car menu, she dialed Veronica's number, humming softly to herself as the call went through.

"Sarah? Her friend answered immediately. "Everything okay?"

"Everything's great." With a smile, Sarah chuckled softly.

"Although I wanted to tell you that I know what you've done."

There was a bit of silence. "What I've done?"

Rolling her eyes, she laughed again. "You don't need to pretend, Veronica. I know it was either you or Deborah or Annie – or maybe the three of you together!"

"Who did what?" There was still a hint of confusion in Veronica's voice, but Sarah only grinned.

"I'm not buying this, so you can stop trying to sound so surprised. I know one of you sent me flowers." She drummed her fingers lightly on the steering wheel. "But none of you needed to do that. Steve already sent me the most beautiful bunch this morning."

"Did he?" Veronica's voice lifted with evident happiness. "That's great. I'm thrilled for you."

Sighing happily, Sarah pulled the car to a stop at the lights. "Thanks. It was very sweet of him."

"So, do you think you'll go out with him again?"

"We're going out again tomorrow night, so please, no more bunches of flowers. I appreciate the thought."

There was another short silence.

"Veronica?"

"I didn't send you any flowers."

Shrugging one shoulder, Sarah chuckled. "Well, that's one down and two more to go. I guess I'll be calling Deborah and Annie. One of you three did it."

"I'm not sure they did." Veronica paused again. "I definitely didn't, and I think they'd have told me if they were up to something like that. We have been doing a little... planning together when it comes to you and your dating life."

"That doesn't sound like you." Sarah tried to laugh but the sound got caught in her throat. "So if none of you three sent me flowers, then who did?"

"I'm afraid I can't help you there. To be honest, I don't

really understand what's going on. First, you're asking me if I sent you flowers and then you're telling me Steve sent you some?"

Pulling the car up to her house, Sarah picked up her cell and climbed out, carrying on with the call. "There's just something a little weird, that's all." Telling herself that she was overreacting again, she shut the car door and headed up to her house. "It's probably a mix up. The flowers must have been for someone else although why one would end up on my car, I —"

Stopping short, she caught her breath, her cell still glued to her ear by sudden perspiration. The tulip she'd picked up on her way out of the house this morning, the one she'd placed on the wall at the end of her driveway was now back of her front door.

But this time, someone had tied a red ribbon around it.

VERONICA

"*H*ey, come right on in. The door's open!"

Hearing the front door shut, Veronica waved one hand as Sarah entered the kitchen. "It's great to see you. Sorry, I'm just finishing up in here."

"No problem." Sarah smiled tentatively. "Nice to see you too."

The four of them usually got together every weekend to laugh and gossip and spend time together. Once, they'd attempted to make it a book club, and, to anyone who asked, that's what it was, but most of the time, they just sat around and talked. It had cemented their friendship, and because of that, just by looking at Sarah, Veronica could tell something was up. "What's wrong?"

With a sigh and a heft of her shoulders, Sarah looked away. "Nothing." Her shoulders dropped. "I had a date with Steve last night."

Oh no. I thought it was going so well. "What happened there? I thought you guys were great for each other."

"We are." Sarah's smile never fully formed. "Don't get me

wrong. We had a great time. I really like Steve, but that's not what I'm worried about."

"Then what is it?"

With a deep breath, Sarah stuck her hands in the pockets of her jeans and looked away. "It's probably nothing, but I can't quite get it out of my head. There was definitely something weird going on with those tulips, especially with that ribbon. I'm sure that wasn't there the first time."

Veronica cleared her throat gently. "The ribbon?"

Sarah's gaze had been drifting across the room, but now it snapped back towards Veronica.

"Sorry. Yes, there was a ribbon around the tulip at my house. It wasn't there in the morning, but it was in the afternoon, *and* someone had moved it from the wall to the doorstep. I know we were on a call at the time – I thought you or Annie or Deborah had sent me those flowers – but I've never explained what happened next or why I was getting myself all twisted up over it." With another sigh, she looked back at Veronica with a piercing gaze. "You solved the mystery of what was going on with the old Draper house, and I guess I'm hoping you can offer *me* some insight."

Veronica's heart squeezed a little. "I didn't do much," she began, only for Sarah to cut her off sharply.

"No, don't do that. You did almost *everything* for that place, even helped catch the guy who killed old Mr. Draper! I think you've got a bit of a gift for solving mysteries, and when it comes to this, well…." Her hands lifted. "There's no one I can really go to. No one official, at least, so I'm coming to you instead."

The knot in her throat was swallowed as Veronica stepped back from all the food she'd been preparing, giving her full attention to Sarah. She sensed her friend needed it. "What's worrying you?"

Sarah bit her lip, then closed her eyes and sighed. "I'm sure it's nothing, and I'm probably overreacting."

"Then tell me everything from the beginning."

With a nod, Sarah continued. "It was after my date with Steve – the double date we went on together. I came out of my house the following morning, and there was a tulip sitting on the doorstep."

A little surprised, Veronica opened her mouth to say something, then snapped it closed again. Right now, all she needed to do was listen.

"It had been cut at the bottom, so one that was taken from a bouquet, perhaps? I couldn't understand what it was doing there, so I picked it up, took it to the bottom of my driveway, and set it on the fence. I figured maybe someone had dropped it, or the wind had blown it up to my house, but there wasn't really much of a breeze that day."

Instead of voicing any concern, Veronica only nodded. Sarah's hands were clasped tightly together, her fingers white, her eyes roving around the room as if she couldn't settle on anything. She'd been carrying this with her for a few days, Veronica realized. A few days where she hadn't said a single thing to anyone. No doubt her worries would have grown significantly since then.

"So what happened after that?"

At the question, her friend shifted a little in her chair. "I was about to get in my car when the mailman spoke to me. He laughed about something — I don't remember what — and then I got in my car and drove to work. A little while later, a bouquet was delivered. A bouquet of tulips." Her gaze finally shifted to Veronica's face. "They were the same color as the one I had found on my doorstep."

Worry began to wind itself into a ball in Veronica's stomach.

"Of course, I thought they were from Steve — that he'd

tried to be romantic or make some sweet gesture, albeit a little misplaced, by putting one at my doorstep! So I sent him a message about this, and he said something about the flowers arriving early, so I figured they were from him — problem solved."

Veronica could see what was coming. "Except it wasn't."

"Except it wasn't," Sarah repeated, rubbing one hand over her eyes. "I got another bouquet a little while later, and *that* was the one from Steve. It had a note and everything. The first one didn't have a single thing – no name or anything."

Letting out a slow, furtive breath so that Sarah wouldn't catch a glimpse of concern, Veronica let a silence settle between them. Right now, something told her that something wasn't right, but what exactly it was, she couldn't say.

"There's more." Surprising Veronica, Sarah closed her eyes and dragged in a breath in an apparent attempt to keep herself calm. "When I got back to the house, the time I was still on a call with you, the tulip I had put on the fence that morning was at my doorstep again...except this time it had a ribbon tied around it."

Unable to help herself, Veronica grimaced, and Sarah's eyebrows lifted.

"You think there's something wrong." Sarah shook her head, her voice cracking. "I knew it. I just knew it."

"Maybe there's some perfectly reasonable explanation." Quickly, Veronica searched her mind for a justification, but nothing came to mind.

"You mean maybe it was Steve? He was just trying to be romantic." From how Sarah ran her fingers through the back of her hair and looked away, her frown growing, it was evident that theory didn't sit well with her. "I can't see it personally."

With a sigh, Veronica shrugged. "Nor can I, although I am

glad to hear you're going out with Steve again. You two really did hit it off."

"We did. He's a great guy." Her smile cracked at the edges before falling apart completely. "Which makes me think it's *definitely* not him. Why would he send me a bouquet after sending me a bunch of tulips?"

"And why would he leave a single tulip on your doorstep and tie a ribbon around it before leaving it there for the second time? That's just someone trying to frighten you, I'm sure of it." Musing aloud, Veronica rubbed at her chin just as the only hint of color in Sarah's face fled. "Sorry," Veronica said, "I didn't mean to put it that way."

"But it *is* creepy." With a slight shudder, Sarah closed her eyes and let out a ragged breath. "Tell me if I'm overthinking this."

"I'm not going to say it's not weird." Thinking it was probably best to tell the truth, she added, "But it doesn't mean there's no legitimate reason behind it. Maybe those flowers weren't for you. Maybe someone made a mistake."

Sarah didn't even attempt to smile this time. "Yeah, maybe."

Veronica could tell Sarah was thinking through everything, from how she gnawed on the edge of her lip. It made Veronica's heart beat a little more quickly than before. Everything Sarah had told her *was* concerning, though she couldn't exactly work out why someone would go to so much trouble over some tulips. What was it about her friend that made someone want to act that way?

"Just telling you has made me feel better." Sarah managed a brief smile and sat up a little straighter. "But I wondered if you could help me work out what's happening – if there is anything going on!" She laughed a little dryly but then rubbed one hand over her eyes. "Of course, now that I've told you, no doubt nothing will happen, and I'll be left only with this dumb story."

Veronica smiled, not missing the slight catch in Sarah's voice. "I'm sure it's probably nothing to worry about. Maybe a case of mistaken identity." It seemed to be the only explanation to offer Sarah some relief, and Veronica went with it even though her thoughts were tumbling over each other. "But come and tell me if anything else happens, okay?"

Sarah nodded and turned just as Deborah walked in with a cheery hello, setting down a bottle on the table. After a few minutes of chatting, Veronica excused herself and headed to her small study.

Something's wrong. I don't know what it is, but something doesn't sit right with what Sarah told me. Last time, Veronica had stepped into danger by choice. This time, she was deciding how much fear to place on someone else's shoulders —and that made every instinct tell her to move carefully.

Opening the door, she stepped inside and hurried to her desk, which sat before a large window. Raking through her drawer, she found a fresh notebook and, grabbing a pen, wrote down everything Sarah had told her. First of all, she wrote the date of her and Chase's double date with Steve and Sarah. Then, on the next page, she wrote down everything Sarah said about what had happened with the flowers. Flipping over the page, Veronica wrote the names of everyone Sarah had recently gone out on a date with.

From what she could remember, there weren't all that many names. First, there had been the pizza delivery guy and the guy who hadn't even shown up. Then there was the farmer — the one who had wanted her to marry him and become stepmother to his three grown-up children and help him on his farm. And after that, there was Steve. Was that all?

I can't miss anyone.

With a grimace, she turned around and returned to the

45

others. Annie had arrived and was busy talking to Deborah while Sarah had gone to pour some drinks.

"Sarah? Can I ask you something?"

"Sure."

Veronica held out the notebook. "I need to know if this is everyone you've dated in the last few months."

Sarah took the pad just as Deborah and Annie came over to join them. Veronica dropped her voice low. "We can talk about this later if you'd prefer."

Glancing at Deborah and Annie, Sarah shrugged. "It's okay." Smiling as Deborah's eyebrows lifted, Sarah gestured to them with her other hand. "I'll fill you guys in later." Taking the pen from Veronica, she dotted one other name down. "I don't think I mentioned him."

"Who is he?" Veronica twisted her head around, trying to read the name. "Jake?"

"Yeah." A flush crept up Sarah's neck. "It was definitely *not* a date but more a one-time... or one-night thing."

Annie giggled, leaning into Sarah. "Oh, really? That's not like you."

Sarah's face burned. "I know, I know. I was so frustrated and upset after my date with the farmer that I wasn't really thinking clearly. He was behind the bar, and we talked for a while. We hooked up, and then I left. That's all there is to it."

Veronica's heart swelled with sympathy for her friend. That was so unlike Sarah. She was always so careful — cautious, even. Every decision she ever made was constantly well thought out.

She must really have been in a bad place after that date.

"And you're not seeing him again?"

"No, he's not really a long-term relationship guy, apparent- ly." Sarah shrugged, her mouth tugging to one side. "It's a shame, really. He was amazing, although Steve is really great too."

The rest of them laughed, but Veronica dropped her gaze to the notebook again. "Okay, so we *might* be able to cross him off the list?" Seeing Deborah's eyes flare, she shrugged. "I'm just trying to work out who Sarah might have got flowers from."

"A secret admirer-type situation?" Annie looked from Veronica to Sarah and back again. "And you've got Veronica to help?"

Sarah hesitated, then sighed. "It's more complicated than that, but it's along those lines."

"Then what about Danny?"

Blinking, Veronica took a few seconds to remember who he was.

"The server from your double date." Annie nodded in Sarah's direction. "You told me about him and how awkward that was. Maybe he really wanted to make sure you remembered him this time?"

It's a good thought. "He was a little forward," Veronica agreed slowly. "Although sending you flowers would be a little unusual, wouldn't it? Especially since you haven't seen him for so long."

Sarah offered her a wry smile. "From what I remember about Danny, he *was* a little unusual."

Returning the notebook to her, Veronica took it and wrote Danny's name on the list. "I've added him here." Holding the notebook out for Sarah to scrutinize again, Veronica waited until her friend nodded.

"Yes, that's everyone."

"Then, at least, that gives me something to start with," Veronica said quietly. "But like I said – and I'll say it again just to reassure you – it'll probably be a mix-up. They probably weren't even meant for you." Giving Sarah what she hoped was a reassuring smile, Veronica jerked her head toward the door. "I'll put this away, and then I'll be right back."

"And you can tell me exactly what these flowers are all about," Deborah murmured, taking Sarah by the arm as Annie followed after them. "It's obviously something that's gotten you worried."

She's not the only one.

As Veronica dashed back into the study to set down her notebook, she bit the edge of her lip, looking down at each name. She wanted to rule out Steve immediately, but something held her back. The truth was, she didn't know any of these guys. Yes, she knew one or two by sight, but for some, she knew nothing about them. She couldn't assume anything. Going to the cops would do no good because what exactly could they do?

So I've got to do something.

Those flowers had frightened Sarah, and as much as she was trying to reassure her, Veronica had to be honest and say it worried her, too. Somebody knew where Sarah lived. Somebody knew where Sarah worked, and someone had set down one of those flowers at her doorstep before sending the bouquet to her work. Had they been watching the house? Had they seen her remove the one from her doorstep and set it on the fence? What had the ribbon been for? Was it made to signify something? Question after question wound around in her mind as Veronica sucked in a breath. Despite what she'd said to Sarah, Veronica was sure this *had* been directed at Sarah. Someone had wanted to catch her attention... and they'd definitely done that.

Veronica couldn't even begin to guess what that reason might be, and that made her all the more concerned.

SARAH

I need to stop letting those flowers get to me.

Sarah rubbed one hand over her eyes. She'd been thinking about the tulips for far too long, and it had already been almost two weeks since they'd arrived at her office. Telling Veronica had been helpful, but it had also meant that her fears had been corroborated. Veronica had done her best to hide her expression, but from how her eyes had rounded, Sarah could tell what she'd been thinking... and it hadn't all been good.

Looking down at her cell, she paused momentarily, swiping through the app. She'd been messaging with one or two other matches, but she hadn't felt the need to plan a date yet. Things were going well with Steve, and she'd be going out again with him soon. Maybe she'd be able to delete that dating app soon, and all of these other worries would just fade away with it.

"Knock, knock."

"Come in."

Jane stuck her head around the door. "Sorry I'm interrupting you."

"That's okay. Not like I was busy concentrating on anything, really."

Grinning, Jane opened the door and walked in. "You've got mail."

Handing Sarah a single white envelope with only her name written on it, Jane shrugged her shoulders in answer to Sarah's silent question. "It was just at the front desk. I don't know who dropped it off or when it came in. I just said I'd take it to you."

"Okay, thanks." It was fairly normal to have different letters coming through the door. Some were from grateful clients, some from less than satisfied clients. Perhaps this was one of those. Sarah opened the envelope.

"Oh, isn't that nice?" Jane smiled as Sarah looked at the card in her hand. On the front, there were two little lady-bugs standing hand in hand, their heads tilted towards each other.

"What does it say?"

Flipping open the card, Sarah read the words, the smile on her face quickly changing into a frown. A lump was in her throat, and a cold hand around her heart.

'Hope you like the flowers. Tulips are my favorite. Wish I knew what yours were. Maybe you'll tell me one day soon.'

"Sarah?" Jane squeezed her shoulder. "Is everything okay?"

Swallowing, Sarah handed the card to Jane, who quickly read it. "What does that mean."

Shaking her head, Sarah took a breath. "I wish I knew." *I'm going to have to tell Veronica.*

"This has to do with the tulips you received last week, right?" Jane's eyes suddenly rounded. "Are you telling me you still don't know who sent them?"

"That's exactly what I'm saying." With a steadying breath, she took the card back from Jane, rereading it. "I don't understand. Who would have sent this? Why not just sign their name?"

Jane smiled thinly. "They already expect you to know who they are." It was so obvious that Sarah's eyes flared as she nodded. "Are you sure you don't recognize the handwriting? Is there anything about it that might give you a clue as to who this is?"

With another tight breath, Sarah pressed a hand to her forehead, surprised at how shaken she felt. She didn't normally get notes like this, and the fact it mentioned the tulips just brought everything she'd been trying to forget straight back to her. "No, and I don't know how I'll find out who it is."

"Whoever it is, maybe once they know you're dating Steve, they'll pull back a little. Obviously, they don't know that yet, but I'm sure if they're watching you, they'll figure it out soon enough."

Even though that was meant to be reassuring, a stone dropped into Sarah's stomach, and she pressed her lips tight together.

"Sarah?"

The door opened again, and before Sarah could say anything to Jane, their boss walked into the room.

"Hi Jane." Her eyes went back to Sarah. "I have a slightly delicate matter to speak with you about." Her eyes went to Jane, who quickly excused herself, throwing a wide-eyed look at Sarah that plainly said, *tell me about this later.*

"Yes, Caroline?"

"As I said, it's something of a delicate matter." Caroline managed to smile, although she stared blankly across the room rather than in Sarah's direction. "Do you remember Mark?"

Sarah blinked. "Mark Hower? The one who changed departments to work with our team? *That* Mark?"

Caroline smiled vaguely. "Yes, that, Mark. I'm afraid he's spoken to me recently about you. He's found you unfriendly and unwelcoming, making it difficult for him to find a happy atmosphere here."

The stone that had fallen into Sarah's stomach turned into liquid, sloshing from one side to the other. "I beg your pardon?"

"It was something about his gift, but you haven't even thanked him yet. In fact, you brushed him off." Caroline waved a hand. "I'm not exactly sure what he's talking about, but I *did* say I would speak to you, and I reassured him you would respond to him promptly."

"I can assure you, Caroline, I have been nothing but considerate to *all* of my colleagues." Her face stung from Caroline's abrupt remarks, and her defenses rose. "I hope you don't believe his statement. This *is* you coming to talk to me about it, right?"

"No, it's not a formal complaint or anything like that if that's what you mean." Caroline made her way back to the door, her job done. "I'm just letting you know what's being said. As you know, we like to have a supportive and engaging atmosphere here, and anything you can do to work on that would be fantastic. Have a great day."

Staring at the closed door for a few seconds, Sarah took a deep breath and let it out slowly, trying to feel only one emotion at a time. As far as she knew, Mark had never really spoken to her before. What sort of gift was he talking about? She couldn't understand it. He'd only been here for less than a month, which meant that somewhere within that time, he'd given her something, and apparently, she'd never said thank you for it. Racking her brain, she looked around the room, only for her eyes to fall on the tulips.

It can't be!

As far as she knew, Mark was a very ordinary guy. He was

around the same age as her. He had a scruffy beard, dark grey hair, and dark eyes. Aside from the beard, he was immaculate with his expensive suits and sharp shoes – so why would *he* send her tulips? Was he offended by her lack of response to whatever he brought?

Her heart slammed into her chest, making her breath catch. Maybe she didn't need to tell Veronica anything. Perhaps the answer had been staring her straight in the face all along. She'd upset Mark. He'd sent her flowers for some reason, perhaps just to be friendly since they now worked in the same department. Somehow, she'd been dismissive and had forgotten to thank him, and he'd gotten all upset by it.

Sarah had spent the last two weeks thinking those flowers had been from some mystery man, getting herself all tangled up in it, but the answer had been right there all along.

It's Mark. It has to be. There's nothing to worry about here.

She started to laugh, only for her smile to freeze in place.

If it was Mark, why would he put a tulip at my door? And why would he do it twice?

First, he would have come to her door before work and set one there, and then, after work, he would have gone by again and set one there for the second time – but this time, with a ribbon around it.

Her heart twisted fiercely, and her breath caught. Perhaps she would have to be careful around Mark until she knew for sure. Aware of the blood pounding in her ears, she lifted her chin and nodded firmly, strengthening her resolve. "I'll go talk to Mark, thank him for the gift, and apologize for not having thanked him sooner." Getting up out of her chair, the door opened, and Jane came in again, murmuring something about extra paperwork for a case.

Sarah sat back in her chair as Jane set a pile of work

before her. Her chat with Mark was going to have to come later.

****

"Got any other plans tonight?

Sarah's heart leaped at the hopeful gleam in his eye. "No, not really."

"Then how about you come back to my place, and I can give us something to do."

Steve's eyes flared wide the second he said it, and he looked away. Coughing furiously, his face turned bright red. "Sorry, that didn't come out right. It wasn't what I meant to say at all."

I wouldn't mind if it were.

Running one hand over his eyes, he glanced back at her and then away again as if he couldn't quite look her in the eyes. "I *was* inviting you back to my place but not because I want… I mean, it's not that I'm not open to that happening, but we could spend a little more time together first. I'm not someone who wants to rush into things. I'm enjoying what we have so far."

Her hand took his. "So am I."

Steve cleared his throat. "Then do you want to come over?"

"I sure do. Even if it's not for *that*." She laughed, and the awkwardness between them broke to pieces. This was their third date, and things were going great so far. They had lots in common; this was the first time he'd invited her back to his place. She wasn't sure she was ready to take their relationship to the next stage yet, but from the sounds of it, Steve wasn't in any rush either. *And that's something of a relief.*

He paid the bill and took her hand as they left the restaurant. Sarah's smile danced across her lips as she looked down at their joined hands. Steve was wonderful, and she was happy. Right now, she could forget about the tulips, forget about Mark, and forget about anything else that might steal away a part of her happiness.

"I'M SO SORRY." Her cell phone kept ringing to the point they'd barely been able to get five minutes of peace. Steve had been great so far, trying to show her around, but her cell had rung three times in the last five minutes.

"Are you sure you don't want to answer it?

"I would but…" She swiped to receive the call, but it ended straight away. "Whoever this is, they only call for a few seconds and then hang up." She could tell Steve was getting irritated, given the tightness about his jaw and the tension lifting his shoulders, and she couldn't blame him for that. After all, she felt the same.

"What if it's an emergency?"

She shook her head. "It won't be. If it were, I'd have a number I recognized flashing up there."

"It's okay. It's not your fault." Steve's smile didn't stretch as wide as before. "Do you want a drink?"

Sarah tilted her head, looking at him, pushing her cell into her pocket. "Maybe I do." The atmosphere suddenly grew warmer as she moved a little closer to him. "What are you offering?"

Steve's eyes flickered. "Whatever you want, I can get it."

"Really?"

Another step had her coming right up to him, and Steve's arms swept tight around her waist. Her hands went around his neck as she tipped her head back, her heart beating faster and faster with excited anticipation. When he dropped his head low, she pressed herself tight against him, her eyes fluttering closed…and her cell rang again.

Steve groaned.

"This is ridiculous." Yanking her cell phone out of her pocket as Steve let her go with a sigh, Sarah hit the answer button and held it to her ear. "Hello? Whoever this is, there had better be a damned good reason for calling me so many times."

Nothing but silence answered her. Her jaw clenched, and she closed her eyes in frustration. Steve shook his head, turning around to enter the kitchen – probably in search of her drinks.

"Hello?" Pulling the cell away from her ear, she checked the screen, but the call was still in progress. Why was no one speaking? "Hello, can you answer me please? You've been calling me for the last hour. What is going on?"

A dull beep told her the call had ended. With a heavy sigh, she followed Steve into the kitchen, where he was pouring her a glass of wine. "So I answered it, but they wouldn't say anything. I have no idea who it was or why they're calling me."

"Maybe a wrong number?"

Her mouth pinched. *Maybe. Although, why did they stay on the call so long?*

"Even if it is, they won't interrupt us again." Pressing and holding the button that turned her cell off, she waited until the screen died, then, showing it to Steve, smiled at him before chucking it onto the kitchen table. "Now, where were we?"

Steve set the wine bottle down, and he was waiting for her as she moved closer. Within seconds, she was back in his arms, his head only a fraction away from hers, his breath hot across her cheek.

A cell phone rang.

Unable to help herself, she let out a quiet scream of exasperation. "How are they still calling?" Angry now, she twisted out of his arms, rushing to the table to look at her cell. "I thought I turned it off."

"You did." Now it was Steve's turn to dig around in his pockets for his cell. "That's mine." With a grimace, he pulled it out of his back pocket, only for his eyebrows to lift. "And it's a number I don't recognize." Holding the screen out to her, Sarah's heart lurched painfully. That number had called her so often that she recognized it immediately.

"Weird." Steve shoved the cell phone back in his pocket. "I'll just ignore it if it rings again." He stepped closer, but the cell phone jumped to life once more. With a groan, he threw his head back, and Sarah stepped away, covering her face with her hands for a second.

This isn't working.

"I'm so sorry."

"It's not your fault." Dropping her hands, she managed a smile. "It seems like someone's determined for us not to have any peace tonight."

"I could just turn my cell off," Steve suggested, but the light wasn't sparking in his eyes any longer. "That would solve the problem."

"Maybe." Her heart sank when he shrugged his shoulders. "Perhaps we should rain check? I'm too tense now, worrying about what might happen next!"

With a sigh, Steve dropped his head and pushed his fingers through his hair just as his cell rang for the third time. With a grunt of frustration, he threw it onto the kitchen table and shook his head. "Okay. I get it. Rain check it is."

"Thanks." A slight shiver ran down her spine.

The two cell phones ringing one after the other was a little... weird. And with the same number, too?

"Maybe next time we turn our cell phones off in advance?" she suggested.

"Absolutely." Even with the cell phone ringing in the background, when Steve kissed her cheek and let his lips burn gently towards her mouth before lifting his head, the urge to wrap herself back up in his arms was almost too much to bear. There was so much expectation in that one small action, but even if she wanted to give in to him, she couldn't. Not now. Too many questions were beginning to pile into her mind, and she wanted to be able to enjoy her time with Steve without any other distractions.

I need to talk to Veronica.

"How about Friday?" Steve smiled, his eyes a little darker than before.

She took a breath. "Friday sounds good." The urge to lean into him and carry on from where they'd left off grew strong, but she shook it away. "I'll let you arrange all the details if that's okay. I picked the last restaurant, so it's your turn."

"Sure. Looking forward to it already."

"Me too." With a smile, she stepped away, although it fell once she walked out of his house and headed to her car. Opening up her cell, she found the number that had been calling both her and Steve, then sent it to Veronica along with a message.

We need to talk. Soon.

VERONICA

"*D*oes she know you're doing this?"

Wincing, Veronica shook her head. "I'm doing my best not to scare her, but I am worried. When she told me about that note at her work, my instincts all went crazy. I think…." Taking a breath, she swallowed the lump forming in her throat. "I think she might have a stalker."

Chase nodded slowly, showing not the slightest bit of surprise. "It does all sound very strange."

The lump in her throat faded as the reality of what she'd said hit her – and that Chase was agreeing with her without question. *Then I'm right. Sarah could have someone stalking her.* "Like I said, I don't want to scare her, but she's my friend, and I promised I'd do what I could to help."

"I get that." Chase smiled and touched her hand. "So now we're getting a coffee opposite the restaurant where she's having a date with Steve, even though it's a little late to sit outside and have coffee."

Laughing, she squeezed his hand. "It's great coffee, though, right?"

Chase chuckled. "It sure is, and it tastes even better since I get to be here with you."

Veronica smiled back at him, her heart suddenly pulling itself away from the worry it had tied around itself the last couple of hours. Chase was *always* a support, always ready to help her out with anything she asked him, ready to go wherever she needed. Whenever she had too much on her mind, he listened until it all of her thoughts got straightened out. *I don't know what I'd do without him.*

"You know I love you, right?"

With a faint look of surprise that melted into a grin, Chase leaned across towards her and kissed her cheek, his breath warm on her skin. "I sure do. And I love you too, by the way." Leaning back, he tipped his head a little. "If the way you helped me is anything to go by, then you'll be a great help to Sarah, too. Do you think she's going to go tell the cops about all this?"

"I think she should but I don't know if she will." Veronica lifted her shoulders, her eyes on the restaurant again. "I think it would be good if they knew because then she could file a report, but Sarah seemed pretty reluctant. After all, it's not that they could do anything. I agree with her on that."

Chase shook his head. "It doesn't make sense. Why would someone want to stalk her?"

"I've been doing some reading on that." Veronica got all twisted up inside, the same way she had when she'd started researching why someone might have a stalker. This situation *was* scary, and what she'd read had been a little overwhelming. "It could simply be an obsession. They might think that she's their soulmate but that she just hasn't realized it yet. It might be a fixation, a belief that Sarah's in love with them, or pure jealousy that Sarah's dating someone else but not them. Or they might want to scare her, to hurt her in some way because of something they perceive she's done to them."

A slight shudder ran through Chase's frame, and he grimaced. "Nasty."

"Exactly. Which is all the more reason I want to keep Sarah safe."

Letting out a low growl, Chase's eyes flickered with a darkness she rarely saw. It only came out when he was mad about something, angry at an injustice, or irritated by something someone had done. "Just so long as you don't get yourself hurt in the process. I'm here for you. You don't have to do this all by yourself."

"I know that." Opening her mouth to say more, Veronica's words stacked up in her throat, her eyes to catch sight of someone she recognized. The pounding of her heart sent adrenaline rushing through her, and she sat a little straighter, her chair scraping on the ground as she pushed it back. "Chase, look. Isn't that...?" Lifting her hand to point, she quickly pulled it back again. With her chin, she gestured across the road. It took Chase a few seconds to realize where she was looking, and when he did, his swift intake of breath told her he'd seen him.

"Yeah, that's Danny."

"What's he doing here?" Leaning across the table as if it might help her get a better look at him, Veronica narrowed her eyes. "Do you think he's looking for her? Is that why he's here? He doesn't work at this restaurant."

"No, he works at the one we had dinner at across town." Chase rubbed his chin but kept his usual relaxed posture, which Veronica hastily tried to emulate. The last thing she needed was to draw attention to herself. "That doesn't say why he'd be here, though."

Chase shrugged. "Maybe there's a simple explanation —

like he's meeting someone for dinner. Let's not jump to conclusions."

Forcing herself back, Veronica swallowed hard and steadied herself. Chase was the one who pulled her back, who helped her to think things through when she was a little inclined to rush ahead. That meant trying to think of all the *other* reasons Danny might be in this part of town, hanging around the same restaurant as Sarah and Steve. All the same, her nerves jangled, and her stomach tightened.

What if I'm looking at her stalker right now?

"Chase. Look." Keeping her voice low and resisting the urge to sit bolt upright or even jump to her feet, Veronica watched Danny move along the sidewalk. He had his hands in his pockets, his head low, but as he walked, he constantly glanced into the restaurant windows. Was he looking for Sarah?

"Okay, so I'll admit he seems interested." Chase shifted a little in his chair. "But then again, maybe he's waiting for someone."

Veronica pushed her chair back. "I think we should go after him." Without waiting for Chase, her eyes fixed on Danny's back as he wandered away from the restaurant. She began to follow after him. "I'm sure he's heading to Sarah's car. She parked it a little further down the road."

"Okay." Without a word of protest, Chase got up, finding her hand so their fingers could lace together. "Remember, we need to act casual. We don't want him to notice us following him."

Veronica didn't respond. Her breath came in short, sharp bursts as she walked down the sidewalk on the other side of the street from Danny. She remembered Sarah saying there had always been something a little unusual about Danny. Was it enough to make him a stalker?

"Slow down a little." Chase pulled her back gently. "I know you're anxious, but chasing after him isn't going to do the situation any good."

"Okay, okay. This is the first time I've ever followed anyone."

Chase chuckled softly. "You're doing a good job. We just need to look like a couple strolling through town, enjoying the evening, so don't squeeze my hand so hard."

He was trying to ease her anxiety, she could tell. "Okay, thanks." Her breath came quicker as she watched Danny move closer to Sarah's car. "But look, he's getting to Sarah's car now and –"

"And there he is walking straight past it." With a smile, Chase slowed his steps. "He's probably here for another entirely different reason. We can go back now, right?"

Veronica shook her head. Something in her gut told her to wait as she yanked Chase back into the shadows. Shoulders lifting with tension and her breath seizing in her chest, she watched Danny as he turned around and meandered back toward Sarah's car. *I knew it. He* is *here for Sarah.*

"Okay, so maybe you were right." Chase's voice was low. "Looks like he's going back to her car."

"Which means that he knows which one it is." Veronica narrowed her eyes as Danny pulled something from his pocket. "Now, what is that?"

"I don't know." Chase wrapped his arm around her shoulders instead. "We can get to it before her, don't worry."

Danny put something underneath Sarah's windshield wiper, then straightened up and looked around, jamming his hands into his jeans pockets again as if he hadn't done a thing.

"Do you think he followed her here?" Veronica struggled to steady her voice, her mind fixing on the possibility she was currently staring at someone who could be Sarah's stalker. "He's leaving. Heading back towards the restaurant."

Chase turned around swiftly. Before Veronica could respond, he had pulled her tight into his arms. His mouth landed on hers in a familiar yet exhilarating kiss, and she responded instantly. She couldn't hold herself back. Chase was the one man who could make her light on fire with a single look. In just a few seconds, every single thought about Danny and Sarah flew from her mind.

"He's gone now," Chase murmured against her lips as she blinked, her vision slightly blurred. "I don't think he saw us."

Slowly Chase's face came back into focus. "What was that for?"

"Because he was coming back this way." Chase grinned. "And because I wanted to." A gentle finger ran down her cheek. "You know I think you're beautiful." He shrugged. "I couldn't help myself."

Aware of the heat in her face, she leaned back into him. "You're very sweet, Chase." Kissing him lightly again, she pulled herself away and turned, letting her gaze slowly swing back toward Danny. "He's walking away."

"Away from the restaurant, too," Chase murmured, one hand on her back. "And he's left a note behind."

Nodding, Veronica took in a deep breath. "Then I guess we should go see what it says."

"SO, WHAT'S GOING ON?"

Sarah paced her living room floor, gesturing wildly. "I'm getting really freaked out, Veronica." Sarah's eyes fixed on hers, but only for a second. "This is something way more serious than last time."

"What do you mean?" Veronica asked, trying to keep her

voice as calm as possible. Veronica gestured to an empty chair when Sarah looked at her again. "Are you sure you don't want to sit down?"

"I'm sure." As if she'd been waiting for the moment, she could tell Veronica everything. Sarah spoke for a long time, her words coming quick and fast. "You know about the tulips. That was the first thing. There was one at my front door when I headed out to work, and then the bouquet of them arrived at my office. When I left the office, there was one on my windshield, and when I got home, the one from the morning had been put back on my doorstep with the red ribbon. Then I got that weird note with no name on it, and then last night..." Her eyes closed. "Someone is trying to get my attention, but I just can't determine who it is or what they want."

Or they're trying to scare you. Keeping those words to herself, the word 'stalker' came to mind, but Veronica kept it back for the moment. "So what happened last night?"

"Yesterday, I had a date with Steve."

Veronica didn't ask how it had gone, knowing this wasn't the focus of the question. "Okay."

"At the end, he asked me if I wanted to go back to his place, and I said yes."

Again, there wasn't a single hint of a smile on Veronica's face, with her growing concern tying a rope around her chest as Sarah continued.

"The second we got to his place, my cell rang. It wasn't a number I recognized, so I just ignored it."

"That's what I would have done, too," Veronica said, hoping to encourage her friend. "So what was the problem?"

"The problem was, it wouldn't stop." Throwing up her hands, Sarah collapsed into a chair as if the strength was gone from her. "Every time I tried to get close to Steve, it would ring and interrupt us. It would only ring a couple of times, so I could never answer it. I could tell he was getting frustrated, so I finally managed to answer it."

Veronica leaned forward in her chair. "And who was it?"

"That's just it." Sarah shook her head. "Nobody answered. I asked them to speak and said a few other things, but there was just silence on the other end. And then they hung up."

Remembering Chase's warning, Veronica moved back and tried not to jump to any conclusions. "Maybe it was a wrong number."

"Except they called Steve after that."

Veronica blinked, the word *stalker* coming back to her mind again and again. It was easy enough to say that the call to Sarah was a wrong number, but that didn't explain why they hadn't responded... unless it was from sheer embarrassment when they realized they'd been repeatedly calling the wrong person.

But that doesn't explain why they called Steve straight after.

"You think I'm right, don't you?" There was a catch to Sarah's voice. "There's something going on. I don't know what's happening, Veronica. I... I'm scared."

"I get that." Dragging in a deep breath, she spread out both hands. "But I can help you. I'm sure I can."

Sarah pressed her lips tight together but said nothing. When she blinked, her eyes grew a little glassy, and Veronica's heart ached. Getting up, she walked across the room and sat on the sofa beside Sarah. "I'm sorry this has happened to you."

"It's really freaking me out." Sarah's hoarse voice soon gave way to tears. "Steve and I were on the verge of a kiss — and the moment just got totally ruined. I don't understand how someone could have *both* our numbers without either of us having them in our contacts. That doesn't make sense."

Agreeing, Veronica let her mind spin over a few ideas.

"Unless they have a way to find out what your cell number is." Seeing Sarah's eyes widen, she sighed. *I'm going to have to say this.* "Sarah, I think there's a big possibility that you have a stalker."

Her friend didn't react in the way she'd expected. There wasn't a swift intake of breath, a look of horror etching itself into Sarah's expression. Instead, there was just a small sigh as her eyes closed tight.

"Have you thought about that yourself?"

"No, not really." The wobble in Sarah's voice said everything. "But it makes sense. I can't think who it would be."

"Or why they'd be chasing you," Veronica added quietly.

"Then will you help me find out why and who?"

Setting her shoulders, Veronica nodded. "We should tell the cops — get them to have a record of your report," Veronica encouraged. "I know I've said it before, but they need to know. It's the only way they're going to have a record of what happened."

"But they won't be able to do anything." Unexpectedly, Sarah reached across and grabbed her hand, her eyes wide and brimming with fresh tears. "I need you to help me with this, Veronica. I can't do it by myself. I'm scared and don't know what's happening."

"And I hate to make it worse, but I have something else to tell you."

Sarah's eyes widened slightly, but she didn't say a word, staring straight back at Veronica.

She took a breath. "I was at the restaurant at the same time as you and Steve." Seeing her friend rear back, she hurried to explain. "I don't mean to say we were *inside* the restaurant. We weren't. We had coffee and cake at this little place across the street."

"Why would you do that?"

"I wanted to make sure you were okay and that no one

came to ruin your date." Veronica put out both hands. "You asked me to look into what was going on. That's what I'm doing. I didn't want you to know in case I put you on edge."

Nodding slowly, Sarah blew out a long breath and closed her eyes. "I'm grateful." Her shoulders dropped. "I just wish you didn't have to do that."

Veronica pressed her lips tight together for a moment to decide her next words. "Sarah? While I was there, I saw something…someone, actually."

Sarah gaped. "Who?"

"Danny." Thinking it would be best to tell her the truth, Veronica told her everything. "He walked outside the restaurant as if he was trying to look for you, and then he put something on your car."

"What?" Sarah's cheeks' tiny hint of color fled as her eyes rounded. "What was it?"

"A note." A frown drew a line between Veronica's eyebrows. "How did he know which car was yours?"

Hesitating, Sarah threw up her hands. "I don't know. Maybe he was watching me when I left the restaurant after our double date?" There was a thin edge to her voice that Sarah understood to be fear. "That's the only thing I can think of."

"It's a good explanation."

"It's undeniably creepy." Sarah shuddered and squeezed her eyes closed again. "What did the note say?"

Getting up and hurrying across the room, Veronica pulled it out from the notebook she'd been using. "Here, see for yourself. I hope you don't mind I took it. I wanted to make sure you'd enjoy your date with Steve without any interruptions."

Sarah's mouth pulled into a scowl. "With my cell phone ringing, it seemed like that wasn't going to happen anyway." Opening the note, she dropped her gaze and read it.

Veronica remained quiet, watching for Sarah's reaction. The note had the logo of the local laundromat on one side of it, and it wouldn't take much to check that Danny had been there that night. The note had been a little unexpected in her mind, and Veronica herself had been surprised. It didn't say much, and it made it very clear that Danny was the one who had put the note on her car. He hadn't tried to hide himself from Sarah, whereas Sarah's other note – and flowers – had been entirely anonymous.

"Okay." Sarah frowned, reading the note aloud. "'Hi, Sarah, it's Danny. Sorry we didn't manage a proper catch-up. I'd love to see you again if you have the time. Here's my number.'" Setting the note to one side, she frowned. "To me, that doesn't sound like a stalker, but it *is* a weird way of trying to get in touch with me. Doesn't he have social media?" She paused, her mouth pulling into a wry smile. "Actually, no, he probably wouldn't. He was always one for being different from the crowd."

"Sometimes an admirable trait." Veronica got up again. "Let me get you something to drink while you think about that note. I gotta say, I agree this isn't how a stalker would act. He's making himself far too obvious, and stalkers don't do that now — from what I understand."

Sarah nodded slowly, but her gaze was already drifting away, no doubt wondering who else it could be if it weren't Danny.

"We can put Steve in the 'no' pile and Danny in the 'probably not' pile." Making her way to the kitchen, Veronica called back over her shoulder. "That's two names off the list." She poured two cups of coffee and added milk and sugar before carrying them back through. Her heart squeezed with sympathy at her friend's expression, pain written in her eyes and into the tug of her mouth. "We're going to work this out, Sarah. I swear it."

"I sure hope so. I'm so grateful to you." With a small smile, she accepted the coffee from Veronica. "You've been so great with this."

"It's no problem." Sitting down, she smiled. "And I hope you have another date with Steve where you don't have to worry about your cell phone ringing."

Sarah laughed, the first time she had since they'd sat down. "Yeah, Steve's a great guy. Maybe I should tell him about all of this." Her smile faded. "I haven't wanted to, but..."

Veronica nodded. "I think it would be good for him to know. He'll be able to support you a little that way."

Picking up her coffee, Sarah took a breath. "I'll tell him when we have our next date." Grimacing, she took a sip. "I just hope he's not going to be too shocked. The last thing I want is for him to drop me because of all this."

"Oh, I don't think he will do that." Looking away, Veronica let her mind run over what Sarah had told her. "And I'm going to do everything I can to find out who's doing this to you. When it comes to your cell ringing – and Steve's cell too – is it possible this person got your number from the dating app?"

Sarah blinked. "Maybe." Looking away for a second, she ran both hands through her hair. "Yeah, in fact, that is probably how it happened. My cell number is on my profile, but it's not meant to be shared with anyone."

"Not unless you chat with them, right?"

It took another moment for Sarah's hands to drop back to her knees. "Right."

"So what if someone was chatting with you and got your cell number that way? They could have done the same for Steve." Veronica tipped her head, seeing how Sarah's cheeks flooded with color. "I won't judge you if you've been chatting to other guys while dating Steve."

"I just wanted to keep my options open," Sarah acknowledged with a sigh. "There's only been a couple, but I haven't arranged a date with them or anything — because things have been going so well with Steve."

"Which makes sense," Veronica reassured. "But if Steve's been doing the same, then you both might be talking to the same person. They might have got your cell number that way."

"I guess." Sarah looked away.

Veronica bit her lip, wondering if Sarah had made the connection. "It also means that this person is pretending to be both a man and a woman." Her shoulders lifted. "That's only if my theory is right, though. It might not be."

"But it's the most reasonable one," Sarah said quickly. "Unless it's someone who knows me and Steve separately – but how likely would that be?"

A tiny smile plucked at Veronica's lips. "Maybe it's Chase."

For just a second, Sarah smiled, but it went soon after, the moment of levity passing quickly. "I doubt it. And before you ask, I don't have those chats anymore. I deleted them all after my date with Steve yesterday. I knew then that I didn't want to try dating anyone new, not when things are going so well between us." Drawing in a heavy breath, she nodded sharply. "So, where do we start?"

Veronica's mind worked quickly. "We've got that list, remember? I can start asking some questions and see if that gets us anywhere."

Sarah's eyes flew wide for a second. "I have someone else you'll have to add to that list." Her hand pinched the bridge of her nose as she shook her head. "There's a colleague of mine, Mark. I don't know what I've done to upset him, but he says I didn't thank him for a gift he brought me – he's new to the department but not the company. He complained to my boss about me."

"What?" Veronica's heart stopped for a second, her eyes widening. "And you think that gift might be the tulips?"

"There's a chance it could be. He could have sent me those tulips, and now he's upset I didn't thank him for that."

"Although that would still make me question why he left one at your door." Veronica frowned. "I guess he would have your cell number, though?"

Sarah nodded. "He could've slipped into my office and pulled Steve's number from my cell." Her brow furrowed. "Although I can't see him doing that."

Considering this for a second, Veronica shrugged. "Maybe." It wasn't the most believable solution to her, but then again, she had to pursue every angle. "Did you say his name was Mark?"

Nodding, Sarah looked at her. "That's right."

"Then, I guess I'll drop in to see you tomorrow at work. Maybe for lunch?" Veronica nudged her friend. "And maybe I'll get to meet this 'Mark.' I've got a few questions I could ask him."

"Really?" Sarah's hand found hers. "Thank you so much for this, Veronica. I don't really have anyone else to turn to."

"You've got me, and you've got Chase, Deborah, and Annie. We're all here to help you. Don't worry, Sarah. We'll get to the bottom of this."

"Thank you."

Veronica smiled. "It's no problem. All I've got to do now is find a way for you to introduce me to Mark."

With a small sigh. Sarah's wan smile pulled the last few hints of color from her face. "I'm sure I can try."

"THERE HE IS."

"Oh?"

Sarah gestured to a man who made his way straight to the

counter. After their discussion last night, Sarah had told Veronica that most of the staff went to grab coffee from the place around the block over lunch, and she was sure Mark went too. They'd been waiting here for thirty minutes.

"I got him." Getting to her feet, Veronica pushed away her nerves and smiled. "I'll go get us a couple of napkins."

Still feeling a tad nervous, Veronica kept her chin up and headed straight towards the counter. "Hi." She smiled and reached for a napkin just as Mark moved forward to order his coffee. "Oh, I'm sorry. Excuse me."

"It's no problem." Mark didn't smile. His jaw was set, and his dark eyes flashed away from her towards the board of drink options. Silently, Veronica wondered how much his expression might change if he smiled.

"Do you work here?" Trying to make pleasant conversation, she smiled when he shook his head.

"No, I work at Sissman and Sons, the Law Firm just around the corner."

"Oh, then you'll know Sarah!" She waited until Mark had finished ordering before carrying on the conversation. "Have you worked there long?"

Mark cleared his throat as the lady behind the counter went to make his coffee. "I moved departments recently."

"Ah, okay." Veronica nodded sagely. "Sarah told me she had a new colleague. I guess that was you."

Mark frowned, his eyebrows furrowing. "Is that right? We haven't said much to each other so far, even though I've been here a month already."

Nodding fervently, Veronica kept her smile fixed in place. "Yes, absolutely. I recognize you. Sarah was telling me something about a bunch of flowers. Tulips, were they?" She waited for a flicker of recognition to cross Mark's face, but none came.

"Uh, no. That wasn't me."

"Oh, are you sure?"

Mark gave no other response, as if he was tired enough already and didn't need to say more. Instead, he looked away and shrugged vaguely.

I guess that's my answer. "Well, it was nice to meet you. I'd better get back to Sarah. Enjoy your coffee."

Walking back to her seat beside Sarah, Veronica's mind turned over the conversation she'd just had with Mark. Either he was very good at keeping his feelings and emotions hidden, or he honestly had no idea what she was speaking about. Her gut told her to go with the latter.

"Well?"

Sarah's wide eyes caught Veronica's attention.

"Nothing, I'm afraid." With a sigh, Veronica sat back down. "I don't think he knows anything about the flowers."

"Really?" Sarah's shoulders slumped as if she'd hoped this would be the right answer. "In a weird way, I wanted it to be him. That way, this mystery and all this worry would end. He definitely doesn't like me, so I thought he might be the one who wanted to try and make my life more difficult."

"Well, it's not him." With a small smile, Veronica tried to sound encouraging. "It's actually a good thing. It's one name off the list, and we can work from there."

"Then you believe him? When he said nothing about the flowers, you think that was genuine?"

Veronica nodded. "Yeah, I do. He seemed to have no idea what I was talking about, so either it's that, or he's brilliant at keeping a blank expression."

Sarah grimaced. "I wouldn't put it past him. I wish he'd just talked to me before he went to the boss. It was so embarrassing having her coming in like that, telling me I wasn't making an encouraging or warm environment." Rolling her eyes, she sighed. "Yes, yes. I know I'm overreacting."

"I get why you're mad." Veronica smiled. "I would be too

– but while I don't think Mark is the one who has been doing all this to you, I'd still keep an eye on him."

Picking up her coffee, Sarah's gaze slid towards Mark as he walked towards the front door. "I can do that." Grimacing, she rolled her eyes. "And I guess I'll have to try and find out what that gift was, too. Maybe that way, we'll know for sure."

SARAH

"*D*anny."

Resisting the urge to wipe her sweaty palms on her jeans, Sarah lifted her chin as she walked into the restaurant. Thankfully, she didn't have to go searching for him. Danny was behind the counter as if he'd been waiting for her.

"Sarah." With a huge smile, his eyes lit up. "You got my note then?"

"Yeah, I did." Aware she was a little on edge, half thinking that Danny might be her stalker, Sarah held his gaze steadily. "I won't pretend I'm okay with you leaving notes on my car. How did you know which one was mine?"

Danny flinched as if she'd slapped him. "You were at my restaurant," he said as if that was an explanation in itself. "It wasn't hard."

"But it's weird." The words slipped from her mouth before she could stop them, and Danny dropped his head, his shoulders rounding suddenly. "Oh. Okay."

"I didn't mean it like that." When his eyes lifted, she closed hers in exasperation, a little embarrassed. "Come on,

Danny, you can't be doing things like that! If I wanted to see you again, I would have come to find you. I knew where you worked. Didn't you think of that?" Her shoulders lifted again. "Or you could have reached out on social media."

"I don't have social media."

Her suspicions confirmed, Sarah sighed and shook her head. "All the same, leaving notes on cars isn't a great thing to do. Someone might get the wrong impression."

Danny's eyes flared, the color vanishing from his face. "Wait, you mean….?" Squeezing his eyes closed tight, he scowled. "I hope I didn't scare you."

Something in her trembled when he looked back at her again. Was that a glint in his eye? Was he secretly hoping she would say yes, she *had* been afraid simply so that he could gain a victory?

"I wasn't scared." Fully aware she was lying, Sarah kept her expression as blank as she could, her eyes looking at his in the hope he wouldn't see any flash of guilt on her face. "But like I'm saying, someone else saw you do that and they were going to call the cops." *That* wasn't a lie at least. Veronica *had* seen him do it and she'd been the one encouraging Sarah to call the cops afterwards. Not because of Danny's note, but because of everything else that had been going on. To her relief, her words hit home as Danny put one hand to his mouth, his eyes huge.

"Oh, no. I didn't even think —"

"No, you didn't." Keeping her tone firm, she rested her hand on the counter. "Danny, you found out where I was for dinner that night. You wrote a note and put it under my windshield blade. What are people supposed to think?"

With a groan, Danny squeezed his eyes closed. "I'm sorry. I took a chance."

"What chance?"

Danny dropped his head a little lower, clear embarrassment written all over him.

"I saw you getting out of the car. I was across the road at the laundromat and when I saw you, I knew I wanted to see you again – just you and me. It's been a long time, and I thought you might... you know, want to spend some time with me too."

Sarah bit down hard to keep her first response from flinging itself towards him. "All the same, there are better ways of doing it, Danny."

A sudden memory flashed into her mind, and she nodded slowly, her gaze drifting to the note with a stamp from the laundromat on the top left-hand corner. Perhaps Danny *had* been there after all. He'd taken a bit of paper from the shop, scribbled his note and taken a chance, just like he'd said.

Less chance of being my stalker, then. A long, slow breath escaped and Danny lifted his head.

"I'm sorry." His voice was small. "I really am."

Convinced now that he didn't have anything to do with being her stalker, Sarah let relief wind through her, her shoulders dropping.

"It's okay, Danny, but like I said, please don't do anything like that again to anyone."

Danny shook his head, fervently. "I won't. I definitely won't." His hand settled over hers for a second, a hopeful light in his eyes. "So what do you say? Do you want to have dinner? Maybe a drink? We could catch up on old times."

Sarah's toes curled and she stiffened. "No thanks, Danny. College was a long time ago and I'm happy to leave that in the past." She spoke gently but all the same, a flash of hurt glinted in his eyes. "Thanks all the same, though." It was the only thing she could think to say, and as she walked away from the restaurant, a heavy weight fell off her shoulders.

She was sure Danny wasn't her stalker, which meant the list was slowly narrowing.

I SURE HOPE I look okay.

It wasn't like her to be nervous over a date with Steve. She was getting to know him better and better, and they still messaged most days about everything from work to cats and what was on at the cinema, which was where they'd been planning to go tonight.

"Hi Sarah, beautiful day, isn't it?"

"It is." A little relieved to have her thoughts interrupted, she smiled back at Joe, the mailman. "Bit late for you to be out delivering, isn't it?"

"Sure is," he chuckled. "There was a bit of a mix-up with the letters and parcels this morning back at the depo, so I had to spend a few hours helping it all get sorted."

"That's real good of you."

Shrugging, Joe smiled but looked away. "It was no trouble."

It's not often you meet someone so generous with their time. "Well, I'm sure they all appreciated it."

Joe waved one hand, chasing her remark away. "Enough about me. How's the dating scene? I remember you told me you had a good night recently."

Oh, great. Trying not to sigh, she sniffed and tried to think of a quick answer that didn't give too much away. "It's been up and down. At the moment, it's on a little bit of an up, but there were some big downers before that."

Joe lifted an eyebrow. "That good, huh?" When she didn't answer, he chuckled quietly. "I had thought about taking a page out of your book and starting dating again. Although maybe it's not going to be as great as I hoped!"

Sarah quickly straightened and smiled. "Just because I

haven't exactly had a ton of success, I wouldn't let that put you off."

Joe rubbed at his chin, his expression a little distant as he looked away from her. "Yeah, perhaps I will. Maybe it's time I start thinking about settling down."

"You'd be able to find someone really quick." She smiled again, reaching out to touch his arm. "You're a great guy. I'm sure you'd have women falling over themselves to get to you."

"Now you're making me blush." With a grin, Joe picked up his bag again and hoisted it over his shoulder, that smile fixed on his face the whole time. "Well, I better go. See you later, Sarah."

Smiling, Sarah headed towards the door, glad to be home. Grabbing for her cell and her keys at the same time, she glanced at her cell, her heart lifting for a second, hopeful that she'd gotten a message from Steve, but there was nothing there. With a sigh, she pushed open the door and stepped inside. There were still a few hours before their date, but it wasn't like him to be so quiet. That in itself was making her a little nervous.

Smiling as her cat hurried over to greet her, Sarah bent down to pet her, her thoughts still on Steve. "It's going to be okay, Snuggles," she murmured to the cat. "Tonight, I'm going to tell him all about my stalker."

HE'D STILL NOT BEEN *in touch.*

Sighing, Sarah tucked her hair behind her ears and searched for her cell phone.

Nothing.

Steve hadn't contacted her all today. Apart from a cheery 'good morning and looking forward to our date tonight' message, it was all she had gotten from him. Yes, he was busy working on a new building at the edge of town, but he usually found time to send her a couple of messages during the day. It wasn't like him to be so quiet. They were meant to meet for their date in an hour – dinner and then a movie. Maybe he'd been so caught up with work that all he'd have time for was to rush home, shower, change, and meet her there.

She nodded. "He's probably just been really busy." Murmuring to herself, she checked her makeup for the third time. She'd gotten ready for their date way too early, but she figured it was better to be early than late. It wasn't that she was nervous about seeing Steve. She was nervous about telling him about the stalker and what had happened so far. She had no idea what his reaction would be. Either he'd want to run from her and end their connection completely, telling her it was too complicated, *or* he'd be supportive and want to help. Whatever he did, it would show her the sort of man he was.

"Maybe you'll get to meet his cat one day." Laughing, Sarah bent down to pet Snuggles again, who had followed after her. Purring, he rubbed his head against Sarah's ankles when she stood up straight, hearing a knock at the door. A little surprised, Sarah went to answer it, glancing at the clock as she went. It was too early for their date, and she wasn't expecting anyone else.

"Steve." Her surprise grew as she opened the door to him. "I didn't think we were meeting for another hour, and I wasn't expecting you to come pick me up." Her eyes ran over him quickly, one hand suddenly clenching with concern. "Unless there's something wrong?" Steve wasn't in anything other than his work clothes. Dust and grime clung to every crease of his pants, and his t-shirt wasn't exactly spotless. What had brought him here straight from work?

"Yeah, I'd say there's something wrong."

He wasn't smiling. When she invited him in, he took two

steps into her hallway, folded his arms, and lifted an eyebrow as if to say that somehow, she knew what he was talking about.

"Are you going to tell me what's going on?"

Snorting, he rolled his eyes. "As if you don't already know."

"I don't understand."

A burst of harsh laughter ripped from his mouth and threw itself at her. "I can't believe you would do this to me." One hand pushed through his hair. "I thought we were getting on great — that we had something which might turn out to be exactly what we were both looking for. Except that's not what you were looking for, was it?" A cold glance flung itself her way as Steve scowled, his jaw working, his eyes narrowed.

Sarah's heart froze in her chest.

"If you'd just told me from the start, then I'd have known where I stood. I would have realized I was into this far more than you."

A sharpness seared the back of her throat. "Steve, I don't understand anything you're saying." Putting out one hand, she touched his arm, but Steve recoiled, his arms still tight across his chest. "Please just tell me what it is that's happened."

"Seems like you hurt someone else already." Letting his hands drop to his sides, Sarah reached for him again but instead, he yanked out his cell phone. "They got in touch with me over the app."

"The dating app?" Confused, she looked at him, only for Steve to roll his eyes.

"You're still playing pretend? Come on, Sarah. He's told me everything about you, stuff I didn't realize until now."

Her confusion grew. It was like a mountain between the two of them. "Told you what?"

"About how you've gone on a ton of dates, looking for one thing and one thing only? That even when you're dating me, you've been messaging loads of other guys, wanting a quick hook-up but nothing more. But you didn't get that from me." His lip curled. "Not yet, anyway."

Sarah's mouth fell open, her eyes widening as horror spread through her. "What? None of that is true. I can't believe you'd —"

"Then explain these."

Blinking to clear her vision of the tears swelling in her eyes, Sarah stared down at his cell phone. On the screen were messages supposedly from her to someone else, messages which she'd never sent. "Those aren't from me."

"Except that's your profile picture right there." Steve jabbed at it with one finger. "No, you don't need to start pulling out your own cell to show me all of your messages. I'm guessing you've deleted them by now. That's not what *I'm* here for, by the way. When I joined the app, I wanted something long-term, something special. I thought that's what we were *both* looking for."

The tears now began to burn. "Please don't do this." Her heart caught, and the ache in her throat grew fierce. "There's something I have to tell you. Something that will explain all this."

Steve scoffed and turned away from her. "There's nothing you can say to explain this."

"I *promise* you those messages aren't from me." Tears were streaming down her cheeks now. "I didn't send them, I swear it."

With a sigh, Steve looked at his cell phone again, then swiped the screen. "And this isn't you either?"

Something sour exploded in her throat, sending a wave of bitterness down into her stomach as she stared at the photos. That *was* her. It was her and Jake, the guy from the bar, standing so close that there wasn't any doubt what she'd been up to...which meant that someone had been taking photos of them as they'd left his bar and walked away together.

"That was before I met you." Her words sounded weak and Steve couldn't even seem to look at her. "This was before I ever went on a date with you. You *have* to believe me."

"I don't have to do anything." Steve cut through the air with his hand. "This isn't the sort of relationship I want, Sarah. If you'd just been honest with me from the beginning, then... well, I guess I would never have asked for that second date."

"Steve, this isn't what I want." Shame burned across her face, and she shook her head, tears still sweeping down her cheeks. "Someone is doing this to me deliberately. Someone is trying to take away the good thing we've got going. They're trying to hurt me. They're trying to hurt *you*."

"Well, they're managing to do that really well, aren't they?" The darkness in Steve's voice told Sarah he didn't believe a word she said. "Don't you get it, Sarah? The proof is right here. You can tell me everything as much as you like, but if I've got these photos and I've got these messages, then what else am I supposed to believe?"

Her throat constricted. What could she say? They had only been on a few dates. It wasn't like they were exclusive or anything, but obviously, he now thought she was someone who only wanted one-night stands before moving on to someone new. And that she'd been doing that with everyone else apart from him.

Maybe that's how I can make him see this isn't all true.

"Think about this, Steve." Tears clogged her throat, pressing her words back behind them, but she forced them forward. "If that was really true, if all I wanted was to have quick flings, then why would I have gone on so many dates with you? Look at me." She gestured to what she was wearing. "I'm all dressed up. Ready for *our* date."

"That's just because you haven't gotten what you want from me yet." The hardness in his voice flooded her with pain. Nothing she could say would make him listen to her. "That's what you want, isn't it, Sarah? You want to hook up with me, and I'm more of a challenge than these other guys. Maybe you expect most men to be that way, but I'm not most men. I'm not going to be another notch on your bedpost, another tick on your list. I want to build something with someone who wants the same things as me."

"And I could be that person." She reached for him again, but he waved her back. "If you just think about this and listen to what I'm telling you, then maybe you might start seeing what I'm saying is true. None of those messages are real, I swear it." All too aware of the desperation in her voice, she moved toward him again, this time catching his arm with both hands. "I *promise* you this isn't me. Those messages have been manipulated, and those photos were from before we dated. I'm not that sort of person. When I was with Jake, I was in a bad place. I had been out on a date and the guy was saying these weird things, wanting me to marry him and meet his grown-up children on the same night! My head was in a crazy place. I don't normally do that sort of thing. You can ask any of my friends — they'll tell you."

For a few moments, Steve said nothing. His jaw worked as if he was trying to figure out in his mind whether or not she was telling the truth. Her heart burned with a furious, desperate hope, but Steve didn't fan it into flame.

Her spirits sank lower. "If you really believe I'm someone who only wanted to hook up with you, then why did I pull back when I had the chance." Her hands curled even more tightly around his arm. "I had that chance, Steve, didn't I? I had turned my cell phone off, and you were going to turn yours off as well. I could have carried on from there, but I didn't. I moved away. I ended our date there. That's not because I just wanted it to be that one night and nothing more. It's because you've begun to mean a lot to me. *That's* the reason I wanted to hold back. I wanted it to be perfect. Don't you understand? There's more to this than you think."

Steve glowered at her. "I'm not sure I believe any of this."

Sarah swallowed hard, tears still on her cheeks. "Please, Steve, please don't push us apart, not when things were going so well. I promise you I'm not that person."

Pausing for a second, Steve dropped his head and let out a huff of air. When he lifted his face to hers, her hands finally fell from his arm. There was a coldness in his expression Sarah knew she couldn't recover from. He'd already made up his mind. The bitterness had already sunk into his heart, telling him she wasn't the person he thought she was. There wasn't any answer she could give him, no explanation she could make that would help him to understand.

"I just don't think it's worth it, Sarah." Steve put his hands back into his pockets, turning away from her towards the door again. "We've only gone out on a few dates, and I really like you, but I think there's more to you than you let show. I can't tell whether you're telling me the truth or pretending, but regardless, I don't think there's any point in carrying on."

She crumpled inside, her heart shriveling. "Please don't believe this. I'm not who they say I am."

With a huff of breath, Steve opened the door, the conversation ending. "I just don't see it, Sarah. Who is going to want to do something like this to you? *Why* would they do it to you?"

His hands fell to his sides, leaving the question hanging.

"I couldn't say." Croaking the answer out, she looked at him for a long moment. "The truth is, I really don't know. I want to be able to tell you. I want to give you all of the answers, but I can't, not when I don't have any for myself." It was as if every word she said piled more burning coals on her head.

With a sigh, Steve turned away, and the door slammed closed between them.

Sarah dropped her head, her shoulders shaking. Putting her head in her hands, she let the tears form around her pain and flood her cheeks. As young as their relationship had been, it had meant a lot to her. The amount of agony that wrapped around her was unexpected, and Sarah fought to fill her lungs with air. It wasn't just the fact that he had ended things. It was the fact he'd believed those messages over her. The horror of realizing that someone was manipulating them, that someone was manipulating *her,* simply to cause her pain, sank into her very bones. She didn't know who he was, but he seemed to be waiting in the shadows no matter what she did.

Is he watching me now? Her heart slammed into her chest as she dug for her cell phone. With blurred vision, she found Veronica's number, her hand shaking as she held her cell to her ear.

"Sarah." Veronica's voice was warm. "Aren't you supposed to be out on your date?"

"Can you come over?" She was crying so hard it was difficult to get the words out. "I have to talk to you. I need a friend right now."

The concern in Veronica's voice was immediate. "What happened? Are you okay?"

"I'm okay." Rubbing at her nose, she wiped her eyes with her sleeve. "Whoever my stalker is, they've got to Steve. He's not injured or anything, but they've poisoned him against me. I don't know what to do. He's gone."

The jangle of keys came through from Veronica's end.

"I'm heading out right now," Veronica spoke firmly. "Hold on, Sarah, I'm coming."

Ending the call, Sarah rested her head against the wall, her eyes closing as fresh tears seared them, fear beginning to creep into the edges of her heart. From the tulips to breaking up with Steve, someone was doing everything they could to hurt her. Shivering violently as a chill ran over her skin, Sarah rested her head on her knees, her arms encircling them. She waited there, not moving till a knock came to the door, and Veronica stood there, flanked by Deborah and Annie. They all stepped inside.

Sarah hadn't moved.

"You're not alone anymore, Sarah." Soon, the three friends were around her, helping her to her feet and taking her to the living room. "We're here," Annie murmured, leading her to the sofa as Deborah disappeared into the kitchen. "We're right here."

Sarah clasped Veronica's hand tightly and leaned into Annie's shoulder. She tried to speak and explain what had happened, but instead, she could only sob. Her friends let her cry, let the pain come washing out of her, but instead of relief, fresh agony came with it. Her world suddenly seemed very small, shrinking in on itself, and as she sat surrounded by her friends, Sarah became incredibly afraid.

VERONICA

"*H*i," Veronica smiled as Chase kissed her on her cheek. "Too embarrassed to kiss me in front of the guys?"

"No." With a grin, Chase lowered his head and kissed her long and hard, one arm going around her waist. When he broke the kiss, she was breathless, and he was laughing.

"Okay, I guess you're forgiven." Taking a few seconds to catch her breath, one hand still on his chest, she smiled at him. "Are you sure you're okay to do this?"

Chase's smile faded. "Absolutely. I hated hearing what happened. Sarah must be really upset."

"I think she's scared." Veronica shook her head, her thoughts returning to how cold and scared Sarah had been a couple of nights ago. "Whoever this is has gone to great lengths to make sure she and Steve don't have a chance. I hate that Steve believed what he saw, but from what Sarah said, those messages and the photos look really legit, although the photos are real, I suppose."

Chase's eyes widened. "So that means someone was

watching her that night. Someone who took photos of her with the bartender?"

"Yep."

"So does that mean you can cross the farmer off the list?"

"Maybe." Her head tilted to one side as she thought. "There's still a chance he followed after her and took photos of her that way, but the likelihood is quite small. I have plans to go to the restaurant and ask if the staff can remember what he did once she left."

"My guess is he waited for his kids." He caught her arm suddenly. "Could be one of them, do you think?"

Veronica paused, thinking quickly. *I hadn't considered them.* "I guess it could have been, but my gut says no. None of them knew what she looked like — although I suppose if one of them wanted her to be their new stepmother, maybe they're trying to make it so Philip is Sarah's only choice."

Chase chuckled a little darkly. "They don't know Sarah as well as we do. There's no way she'd ever go marry a retired farmer."

"All the same, I should consider that." Veronica reached up to kiss his cheek, mentally reminding herself to put that suggestion in her notebook. "Thanks, Chase. It's getting so complicated. I've made a list of everyone Sarah dated the last couple of months, but so far, all I'm doing is taking people *off* that list – or moving them to a 'maybe' pile – one after the other."

"Isn't that a good thing?"

Sighing, she nodded. "Yeah, I suppose. It just feels like it's taking forever. I'd rather find the responsible person's name instead of having to go through everyone else one by one."

"Maybe that's just how things have to be right now. It's good you've managed to get some people off the list. Don't beat yourself up about not being able to find the right person so far."

Closing her eyes tight, Veronica pushed back the heat that grew behind them. "The truth is, I'm scared about what the stalker will do next. I haven't said anything to Sarah, but I can see things are escalating. First of all, there were the tulips. Then there was the note. Now he's been calling her *and* calling Steve. He's determined to get her all to himself one way or the other. If that's his motivation, it seems to me like he doesn't want her to be paying attention to anyone else apart from him."

"But how is she supposed to do that if she doesn't know who he is?"

Veronica opened her eyes to see Chase looking back at her, his soft expression calming her fears. "Does he want her to guess? To work it out? I don't know." Her shoulders lifted, then dropped. "I guess that's what makes him a stalker."

And I have to find him quickly.

"Well, let's go see if you can get some help with that."

Chase jerked his head to the front of the house. Most of the construction workers had been moving around outside, but there were a few inside as well. "I called a friend this morning. He's the foreman on this job. He said Steve was already in, so let's go. Hopefully, he'll talk to you."

Reaching up, she held him close for a second. "You're the best, Chase." His strength supported her and helped her build her own when she was weak. "I don't think I could do this without you."

"I'm sure you could." Chase's confidence had her smiling. "But I'm glad to be here with you. Come on, let's go talk to Steve."

"OH, HI." As Chase spoke to the foreman, Veronica waved one hand at Steve, hoping she'd painted on a surprised expression. "Great to see you again, Steve."

"Yeah, hi." Steve didn't look in the least bit pleased to see her. In fact, he was frowning, his face already a little sweaty from whatever it was he'd been doing.

"Sorry to interrupt you." Veronica gestured towards Chase. "Chase had something to do over here today, and I thought I would tag along with him."

"Right." Steve folded his arms over his chest. "I'm guessing Sarah's told you everything."

She blinked. He was as direct as Sarah could be sometimes, which was probably one of the reasons they got on so well. "Yeah, she has." With a breath, she threw out both hands. "Steve, you're genuinely making a mistake. I know Sarah. I've known her for a long time. She's one of my closest friends, and I can guarantee whatever you were sent wasn't from her."

Scowling, Steve let out a sharp exclamation. "Did she send you over here to say that to me?"

"No." Catching the anger burning in his words, Veronica took a breath. *I need to stay calm.* "But she's my friend, and I hate seeing her so upset. She really likes you."

For a second, Steve's expression softened, the narrowing of his eyes faded, and his jaw slacked a little. "I really liked her too." With a sigh, he looked away, turning his head so he didn't have to glance in her direction. "But I know what I saw. That guy was trying to warn me about her, and I'm glad he did."

"Except maybe he was trying to push her *away* from you." Putting one hand on her hips, she tilted her head. "Have you ever thought about that?"

From the way he frowned, Veronica was sure he hadn't. Bringing in a little boldness, she moved closer to him, forcing him to look into her face. "What if it isn't the way you think? What if Sarah's been telling you the truth? What if

I'm telling you the truth? Whoever sent you those messages had their own reasons for sending them."

"I can't imagine what those reasons would be." Steve rubbed one hand over his chin. "Unless it's one of those other guys that she dated. Maybe they wanted more from her, and now, since she's not giving it to them, he's trying to get his revenge."

"Which would make him downright cruel," Veronica countered. "But I swear to you, Sarah's not like that. I'm not saying she didn't hook up with Jake from the bar, but he's been the only one, and that came after a terrible date with Phillip."

"Which was when we were between dates, according to the photo."

"And the photo is wrong," Veronica insisted, trying to stop her voice from rising. When he didn't instantly respond, she took another step closer, forcing him to listen to her. "Listen, I know Sarah. I was as surprised as anything when I heard about Jake because I know that's not like her, and then she went on to meet you. You can't be angry about someone who came before you, can you?"

This seemed to throw Steve off because he immediately dropped his head forward and shrugged, saying nothing.

"Would you like her to get mad about whoever you dated before her?" Her words were fixed and steady. "I get you believe those messages, but I'm telling you they're not from her. The photos might be legitimate, but the date on them is wrong. Whoever sent them to you has an ulterior motive – and they've succeeded in hurting you and Sarah."

Steve made a low noise in the back of his throat and rubbed one hand over the back of his neck.

Feels like I'm getting through to him. "I give you my word. Sarah didn't do what those messages say she did. I understand you don't know her all that well yet, but I do."

"I thought I was getting to know her."

"And you are." Seeing the flicker in his eyes, she touched his arm. "Steve, listen to me. Don't throw away something that could bring you so much happiness. You don't even know who sent you those messages. It could have been anyone. What makes you think they're telling the truth?

"Because…" Blinking, Steve cleared his throat. "It's just a guy thing. One guy looking out for another."

"I think that's a little naïve." Trying to speak carefully to avoid pushing him away, Veronica dropped her hand back. "Think about Sarah, think about what you know about her, and then think about this other person who's been in contact with you. Of the two of them, wouldn't it make more sense to trust the person you've met — the person you know over someone who hasn't even shown their face?"

Steve rubbed one hand over his eyes. "Maybe."

Finally, "There's more to this, Steve. It's not my place to tell you, but I think you should listen to Sarah if you get the chance."

A slight frown danced across his forehead. "You mean to say that everything she was saying is true?"

"I believe it is." Veronica held herself straight, looking back into his eyes. "There's been some strange things going on, and she's really scared. After what happened with you and these messages, I'm also beginning to get really concerned."

Steve ran one hand through his hair, making it stick up in all directions. His eyes were wide, and he suddenly had gone a little pale. "Oh no. I didn't…. I don't…."

"Do you mind if I see those messages?"

It took him a few seconds, clearly a little shocked by what she'd told him. "I deleted them. I did take screenshots, though. I can send them to you?"

"That would be great." Pulling out her cell, she quickly

gave him her number. "And I hope you don't mind me coming to speak to you about this. Sarah is my friend, and I want her to be happy." She pushed her smile upward a little more. "So far, you seem to be making her happy, Steve."

He let out a half laugh, half groan. "Right up until the moment I told her I didn't believe a word of what she'd said and that I didn't know who she was anymore." The color slowly began to return to his face, except that it pushed red heat into his cheeks this time. "I don't understand everything that's going on, but if you're telling me something more is happening, I believe you. I believe *her*. Like I should have done from the beginning."

A great swell of relief lifted her heart. "I'm glad to hear it." Putting out one hand, she waited for him to shake it and smiled when he did. "And remember to send me those screenshots, will you? It's important I look at them."

Steve gripped her hand before she could pull away, his gaze holding hers. "I thought you were a real estate agent."

"I am." Veronica smiled at him. "Why?"

"Because you sound much more like a private investigator." Letting go of her hand, his eyes still watchful, he nodded slowly. "Do you really think that you can help her with this?"

"Yes, I do – and you can too." With a firm nod, she turned around, walking back towards Chase. That had gone better than she'd expected. Only a few probing questions had helped Steve realize there might be more to these messages. He probably hadn't been in the right state of mind to listen to what Sarah had to say at the time, but nonetheless, she was grateful that he was now ready to hear what Sarah had to say. Hopefully, she would tell him everything.

"All done?" Chase slid one arm around her waist as Veronica nodded, blinking in the bright sunshine.

"Steve's going to be okay. He has some thinking to do, but he'll get in touch with Sarah soon, I think."

"That's good." Chase's rough cheek scratched hers as he leaned to kiss her, but she didn't care. All she wanted to do was wrap herself up in him and let the stress of the last few minutes melt away.

"He's going to send me those screenshots, too." When Chase lifted his head and looked at her, she explained again. "The screenshots of the messages he was sent."

Chase's mouth tugged to one side as he looked at her. "Do you really think you can find something out from them?"

With a sigh, she shrugged and turned away, heading back towards the car. "I don't know, but I have to try."

"And you can ask Annie if you get really stuck," Chase reminded her. "She works in the police department."

"As an IT specialist," Veronica reminded him with a chuckle. "But yeah, I guess if anything came up, especially with those cell phone numbers, I could ask her for help. It might have to become an official investigation, though. I just have to get Sarah to report this to the police first."

"Maybe after this, she'll do it," Chase murmured as they left the construction site. "This has really scared her."

And it has scared me too.

"There he is."

Veronica eyed Phillip. He'd been easy enough to find once Sarah had given her the name of his farm. A quick search had brought up his picture, farm, and shop easily enough.

"Okay, so there's two of them here." Veronica's gaze darted towards Phillip, then to the young man behind the counter. "You go talk to Phillip, and I'll take on his son."

Chase frowned. "How do you know it's his son?"

"Because he looks like him." With a shrug, Veronica smiled when Chase grinned back at her. "Just talk produce and see what you can get out of him that way."

Chase's grin slipped. "I'm not sure I'm the best person for this, but okay." Jutting out his chin, he wandered across the shop floor to where Phillip was standing, sorting out some potatoes in a large, green box.

Except fresh produce wasn't really why she was here today. All she wanted was answers.

Picking up her basket, she put a few things in and then went to the counter. She had to admit that even if Phillip wasn't the greatest guy in the world, his produce looked and smelled incredible.

"Hi there." She smiled at the young man behind the counter. "I'd like to purchase these, please."

"It's a great selection!" He smiled, and Veronica smiled back. "Let me just get this put through for you."

"Thanks." Leaning on the counter with one elbow, she gestured to the rest of the shop. "I've never been here before. Have you been running it for long?"

"About fifteen years, although my dad runs the place right now. I'm going to take over soon. My dad and his wife will run the place for a while alongside me to make sure I know what I'm doing, but eventually, I'll be taking over full control. My younger brother is going to be on side as well, so hopefully, there'll be a lot of good produce for many years to come."

"That's great." *Wife? What wife?* Was Phillip still expecting Sarah to come and marry him? "So, your mom and dad are both close to retiring?"

The young man laughed and shook his head. "My dad sure is, but his fiancé ain't so much. But that's okay. He needs someone to look after him. He's been living most of his life alone ever since my mom passed away."

"I'm sorry to hear that." Veronica's expression of genuine sympathy reached out to him, but the young man only shrugged.

"It was a long time ago. I don't really remember much about her, but I'm glad Dad's happy now. We'll have a big celebration after the wedding and then some big discounts at the store, in case you want to come back again soon."

Veronica grinned at him. "Thanks, I'll make sure to do that. When's the wedding?"

"Next month." Laughing, he shook his head. "Can you believe it? My dad met someone new and found himself engaged in only three weeks."

Blinking, Veronica's doubts began to rise that he was talking about Sarah. *I think she'd know if she was engaged.* "That's nice." She managed another smile. "What's her name?"

"Alice." He smiled. "She's going to be really good for my dad, I can tell."

The heaviness lifted from her shoulders the next second as she took a long breath. He hadn't said Sarah — he'd said Alice. "Well, I'll make sure to come by again soon." She smiled warmly. "Thanks."

"PHILLIP DIDN'T SAY MUCH." Walking back towards her at the parking lot, Chase threw up his hands. "He kind of clammed up."

"He's engaged, and his fiancé's called Alice." Laughing when his eyebrows lifted, Veronica pressed herself on her toes to kiss him. "I'm surprised he didn't tell you much, though. Maybe he's more open on his dates."

"Maybe." Phillip smiled at her. "All the same, it's good we don't have to worry about Sarah."

With a nod, Veronica smiled, only for it to run into a frown. "Which means we might be in a bit of a bind."

Chase blinked at her. "Why?"

"Because who else is left on the list?" Running one hand

over her face, she closed her eyes tight, a sense of panic tightening her chest. "It's not Phillip. It's not Steve. It's not Danny. I still have to see Anthony, but if it's not him, then…"

"It's got to be Jake." Chase shrugged. "You've found the answer.

"I don't see how it could be. He didn't know anything about Sarah, and that was what he wanted. They didn't meet until that night at the bar."

"Unless they met before, and he was frustrated she didn't remember."

Thinking for a few seconds, Veronica let out a slow breath. Her instincts told her it wasn't Jake, so she shook her head. "I don't think it is. It wouldn't make any sense. Why would he do all of this to Sarah if they've already hooked up *and* if he's busy now pushing her away? Her stalker, whoever it is, wants to be with her. He's obsessed with her, telling her there's no one else in the world better for her than him. So why would he say he only wants a one-night stand if he had that chance? That doesn't add up, so I don't think it is Jake."

With a sigh, Chase shook his head. "Yeah, you're right. It doesn't. So if it's not Jake and it turns out Anthony's in the clear as well, then who are we left with?"

Veronica tried to come up with an answer and tell Chase what suspicions she had, but her mind drew a blank. "I need to get back to look at the list. There must be someone — or something — we've missed out. Or maybe it'll turn out to be Anthony, and then it'll all be over."

SARAH

*Y*ou *have missed a parcel. Please call to arrange redelivery.*

Muttering, Sarah shook her head and then dialed the number on the card. "Hi there, I've got a missed parcel I need to have redelivered?"

The man on the other end asked for a few details and soon confirmed that the parcel would be on its way to her. She had no idea what the parcel was, but then again, maybe she didn't need to know. She hadn't ordered anything. Perhaps one of her friends had sent her something as a surprise, just to cheer her up.

Once the call had ended, Sarah glanced at the clock, then let out a stifled exclamation. She was supposed to be at Deborah's place already and she hadn't even changed her clothes yet.

Looks like I'm going to be a little late for dinner tonight.

"I THINK you should go out again. Date someone new."

Sarah rolled her eyes. "Why? And with who? In case

you've forgotten, all of my dates so far have ended up being nothing but trouble."

"All the more reason to get back on the horse," Deborah grinned. "How about that cousin of mine? You know I've mentioned him before, and I *still* think you'd get along great."

"And what if we don't?" Sarah planted her hands on her hips as Annie poured them all a drink. Veronica had yet to arrive, but the three of them were getting ready for their fake book club all the same.

"Then nothing?" Looking a little confused, Deborah shrugged. "Why? What do you think would happen?"

"I think there's a risk it could damage our friendship," Sarah told her plainly. "If things don't work out then…"

Deborah shook her head and waved one hand. "That wouldn't happen, so don't let that put you off. I don't care if you guys hit it off. If you don't, then that's okay. And if you do…well," she grinned, light dancing in her eyes, "then you might end up being family one day."

Annie snorted with laughter, and Sarah couldn't help but join in. "You see, that's the sort of pressure I don't want!"

"You know I'm kidding." Deborah smiled and reached for her glass. "But all the same, he's there for the taking. All I've got to do is call him, and he'll be happy to go out to dinner with you. I know he's looking for a good woman, and *you're* a good woman."

A small smile crept across Sarah's face at the compliment. "Thanks." Her hand settled on her throat. "I just wish Steve thought so."

Her friends had been filled in on exactly what she had done and what was being said. They had murmured with sympathy and, at the same time, expressed their frustration with Steve and his lack of trust in her.

"Steve *should* think so. It's almost like he doesn't know you at all," Annie said, waving one hand. "Of course, you're not that sort of person. He shouldn't believe those messages."

"I'm genuinely not," Sarah replied with a sad smile. "That thing with Jake was just a one-night stand which is *so* unlike me."

Deborah put one hand on her arm. "That man's not going to realize what he's missing until it's too late. But in all honesty, I think going out for a quiet dinner with Justin might be a good thing for you. Maybe take your mind off things a bit."

Sarah hesitated and shrugged. Justin definitely *couldn't* be her stalker because she'd never met the guy before. He lived in the next town, according to Deborah, so maybe her friend is right. Maybe there was no reason for her not to meet someone new.

She took a breath. "Okay."

Deborah blinked. "Wait, are you sure? A minute ago, you were pushing me away from the idea."

Sarah nodded. "Yeah, I'm sure, although he should probably show me a picture of him first so I know who to look for!"

Beaming at her, Deborah turned her attention to her cell. "He's actually on the same dating app as you." Beginning to sweep through her photos, Deborah narrowed her eyes a little, looking for a photo. "I'm surprised you haven't matched yet, actually."

Sarah curled her lip and growled. "I don't think I'm going to touch that dating app again. I've had nothing but failure — apart from Steve, of course." It was like a punch to her gut mentioning his name, but she quickly drew in a sharp breath, pushing the pain away.

"But you're still on it, right?" Annie propped one hip up against the counter, drink in her hand. "Or have you decided to quit again?"

Sighing, Sarah shook her head. "I've got it on my cell, but I haven't used it. I've been so mixed up with everything I haven't really had a chance to think. I'll be honest, ever since there was a suggestion that my stalker was using the dating app to get in touch with me and Steve, I've been reluctant to go back to it."

Annie's face filled with sympathy, her eyes rounding just a little. "I can understand that. Sorry, I should have realized."

"You know we're all really sorry for all the trouble you've been having," Deborah added, still scrolling through her photos. "And if you ever need anything – even a place to crash for a little while, then you know my door's always open."

"And so is mine."

Sarah smiled at both of them. "Thank you. I appreciate that so much." Settling one hand against her heart, she took in a deep, steadying breath. Even with all of the worries about her stalker and the anxiety that came with it, and the upset over Steve, she still had good friends, and that was something she could be grateful for.

"Ah-hah!" Changing the subject back to her cousin, Deborah grinned, holding out her cell for Sarah to see. "When should I tell him you're free?"

Looking at a smiling man, his eyes lit with laughter and his arm slung around Deborah's shoulders, Sarah hesitated. *Am I really doing this?*

"Sarah?"

Yeah. I am. "Wednesday?"

"Great, I'll tell him." Before Sarah could even think to regret what she'd said, Deborah was busy typing a message. Taking a sip of her drink, Sarah watched her friend's fingers fly over the cell screen and hoped she was making the right decision. *Maybe I should have waited until all of this calmed down before I started thinking about dating again.*

Her frown grew quickly. The last time she'd decided that, she'd stopped dating for months. She probably would have kept holding back if her friends hadn't convinced her to start up again. No, she wasn't going to let this stop her. Yes, Steve had hurt her. Yes, she still really cared about him and wished it was him she was going out on a date with instead of this Justin, but hey, she had to start over somehow – and it looked like Justin was going to be the one to help her do that.

THE RINGING of her cell caught her attention, but Sarah quickly ignored it. She was on a date with Justin, which meant giving him her full attention, not her cell.

"Do you want to get that?"

A little embarrassed, she shook her head, glancing at her cell screen – only for her heart to come to a dead stop in surprise.

Steve.

The sudden urge to answer it, to see what he wanted, rose up high, but with an effort, she turned her notifications to silence and gave her full attention back to Justin. "Sorry about that. It's off now."

"Great." Justin's easy smile helped pull her mind away from Steve's call.

"So tell me a little about yourself."

They'd already talked about her, her job, her life, and her cat, with the latter part of the conversation bringing a slight surge of disappointment that he didn't have a cat himself, but then again, that only reminded her of Steve. It had been one of the things they'd had in common, and she had loved that about him. In her mind, a man who owned an animal like a cat had a gentle heart.

"Not much to tell, really." Shrugging, he grinned at her. "I work in finance, which sounds a lot grander than is. Basically, I work in the bank in town as a financial advisor."

Laughing, she smiled back at him. "So not like one of those big money guys in the city."

"No, not like that at *all.*" They laughed together again, and Sarah found herself relaxing. Deborah had been right. Her cousin was a nice guy.

"My parents live in the city, though, so I visit them occasionally. I've got one brother, but he lives in Alaska, and that's about it, really." He smiled. "Not much else to tell."

"I'm sure that's not true," Sarah challenged gently. "I bet you have hobbies, interests, things like that." Her smile lifted. "Maybe we share some."

Justin's eyebrows lifted as if he hadn't expected her to be so encouraging. "Maybe we do. Do you like baseball at all?" Laughing when she made a face and shook her head, he let one shoulder raise a little. "That's okay. We're bound to find something in common."

Settling into their conversation, Sarah's heart softened at the kindness in his eyes. "I'm sure we will."

They ordered, and the conversation flowed easily enough. Sarah had to admit that Justin was easy on the eyes, what with his shock of dark hair, easy smile, and vivid green eyes. *And the tight shirt isn't too bad either.* The food arrived, and she was just about to pick up her fork when the server came over again.

"I'm sorry to interrupt you before you've even started." Smiling apologetically, she held out a bouquet to Sarah. "This arrived with the instruction to be given to you immediately." Her eyes went to Justin, smiling warmly at him as though he was somehow responsible for the bouquet of tulips that was being held out to Sarah.

Her mouth went dry. *Tulips?*

"Oh, and here's the note that came with them, although

why you needed one, I don't know." The server giggled and moved away, leaving Sarah staring at the bouquet of tulips in her hand and the note on the table beside her.

"Unfortunately, these aren't from me." Justin's smile grew a little fixed, the sparkle gone from them. "Unless you're planning on going on a second date with someone else after this?"

Sarah shook her head, struggling to come up with any explanation. "I don't... I don't know who they're from." That was the truth, at least.

"Well, you could always open the note." Justin gestured to it, then smiled. "Maybe that will give you a clue about your secret admirer."

Her laugh dried in her throat. "Yeah, sure." With hands that shook slightly, Sarah picked up the note, setting the tulips down. "Just give me a second." Unfolding it, she reads the short lines, her stomach rolling with fear.

'Steve wasn't good enough for you. This guy isn't either. Sooner or later, you'll see I'm the only one for you. By the way, you looked gorgeous today. I loved that green dress.'

She couldn't see clearly anymore, the words blurring as she took in short, sharp breaths that sent pain through her chest.

"Sarah." Justin unfolded his arms and put one hand over hers. "Is everything okay? You've gone white as a sheet."

"I'm... I'm fine." Forcing a laugh, she resisted the urge to rip up the note, sliding it into her pocket. "It's from Deborah. I guess she really wants this to go well."

At this, Justin immediately laughed and rolled his eyes, his grin quickly returning. "That sounds like Deborah," he told her, although his voice seemed to come from very far away. "You just looked really shocked. I thought that –"

"Oh no, nothing's wrong." Getting up from her chair, she gave him a brief smile. "Excuse me for a second. I'll be right back." Picking up the tulips on her way, she caught his frown. "I'll see if the front desk can hold them until I'm ready to go home." Without another glance, Sarah made her way to the front desk on shaking legs, as if every part of her was slowly breaking into pieces and shattering on the floor. "Here," handing the tulips to the man behind the desk. "Please give these to someone else — one of your staff, perhaps. I don't want them."

Without giving him a chance to argue, Sarah turned sharply towards the front door, only to walk straight into someone solid. Catching her breath, she looked up, ready to apologize, and blinked in surprise.

"Sarah." Jane took a step back, her cheeks a little flushed. "Are you okay? Sorry, I didn't mean to –"

"Jane." Seeing a familiar face suddenly brought a huge swell of relief. "No, it was my fault. I was heading outside for… for fresh air." She took a deep breath. "So, what are you doing here?"

"Got a date!" Her colleague laughed, making Sarah smile. Something about her seeing Jane here, outside of work, eased some of her fright. "After seeing the flowers you've been getting, I figured I'd try and start dating again. So, here I am!" Her hands flung up and then dropped down again. "Although I'm *really* early."

"Better than being late!" Her heart began slowing its frantic rhythm as Jane smiled big and bright. "I'm really pleased for you – but you should have told me!"

"I was a little…" Jane shrugged and looked away. "It's been a while, and I'm just hoping this goes okay."

"I'm sure it will."

Jane's eyes twinkled. "And if it doesn't, there's plenty more to swipe through, right?"

"Right."

The smile slowly slipped from Jane's face, and she put one

hand on Sarah's arm. "Are you sure you're okay, Sarah? You don't seem like yourself."

"I'm... I'm fine." Taking a deep breath, she smiled back at her friend. "That's the thing with blind dates – it can get a bit overwhelming. Seeing you here has helped calm me down."

Jane's expression softened. "I'm glad to hear that. You know where I am if you need to escape, right? Just send me a message, and I'll call you with an emergency."

Laughing, Sarah shook her head. "I'll be fine, thanks. Justin's great."

With a giggle, Jane grinned back at her. "Then I guess I might be calling *you* if this date doesn't go well!"

"Let's hope it does, right?"

Jane smiled and then stepped forward to hug Sarah tight. "Thanks. Let me know how it goes, okay?"

"Okay. See you later." With a smile, Sarah stepped outside, giving a quick wave to Jane and then taking in a long breath of fresh air. Her heart was still beating a little too quickly, but it wasn't the furious clamor it had been before. Seeing Jane had helped that, and she appreciated how quickly she'd been able to relax.

All the same, I need to call Veronica.

Taking the note out of her pocket, she held it before her and took a photo, ready to send it to Veronica.

How did my stalker know I was going to be here?

Had whoever this guy was been watching her? Noting everything she did? Did he have access to her cell phone somehow? Her eyes closed. *First thing tomorrow, I'm going to change my number.*

"Hey." Justin stepped up to her, his smile gentle. "You're not okay, are you?"

Sarah swallowed hard, her head lifting sharply from her cell. "Sorry, I'm being a terrible date."

"Any reason why?"

With another breath, Sarah pressed her lips together. "It was the flowers. They just threw me."

Justin put his hands in his pockets, his elbows sticking out. "Can I ask what it was about them?"

Licking her lips, she hesitated. *How do I explain this?* "I had a bad experience, and they just reminded me of that."

"Okay." Justin shrugged, smiling at her. "If you need to go home, that's alright with me. We can reschedule."

Her heart melted a little. "You'd really be okay with that?"

"Of course." His smile reached out to her. "Whatever you need."

He really is a nice guy. Shame that this date's been ruined by those flowers. Swallowing hard, she shoved her cell back into her pocket. *Or I can choose not to let it.* "No, let's go back inside. I just hope my pasta isn't too cold."

Justin blinked, then smiled. "Are you sure?"

"Yes, absolutely. Thanks, Justin."

"No problem." Moving to the door, he held it open for her, and after a brief pause, Sarah lifted her chin and walked back into the restaurant. She wasn't about to let this stalker ruin her date. If he *was* watching, he would see her walking straight back to her table, sitting down with Justin, and enjoying the rest of her meal. He would see she wasn't going to be pushed away or be knocked under by what he was doing. Steady determination began to eat away at her growing fear, and she picked up her fork. Sarah allowed herself a grim smile. *I'm not going to let him beat me down. He's not going to win. Maybe this way, he'll realize that.*

VERONICA

*V*eronica logged into the dating app, wincing as she did. After Steve had sent her those messages, the only way she could search for the user was to log in and set up a profile for herself. On top of that, she'd found Anthony still on there as well and now had plans to make her way to the pizza place to see exactly what he had to say for himself.

"Hey. What are you up to?"

"Oh, just getting myself a date."

When Chase stopped dead, his eyes wide, she couldn't help but laugh. "Nothing you need to worry about, though."

"I beg to differ." Chase walked towards her. "If a man comes in to hear his girlfriend say she's getting herself a hot date, he's going to need more details."

"Not if his girlfriend is doing what she can to help out a friend." When she turned her head, Chase was staring down at her cell and, laughing, she leaned up to kiss him. "You've got nothing to worry about."

"That's a relief." Chase's second kiss lingered. "You gave me a fright there for a second."

"I didn't mean to." Still smiling, she took in a deep breath and then gestured to her screen. "Here are the screenshots that Steve sent me, and here is the account of the guy who sent them." Swiping, she saw Chase's eyes widen.

"Okay. So this, 'SnakeEyes173' is still active?"

"It looks like it. See here?" She pointed to the top right corner. "It tells you when they were last active, and he was busy here yesterday. Plus, I found Anthony on here too. I'm planning to head to his pizza place tonight."

Chase nodded slowly, one hand rubbing his chin. "Does *SnakeEyes173* have a profile photo?"

"Yes." Rolling her eyes, she found it for him. "It's obviously a stock image. So it doesn't look like I can get much out of him from this. My plan was to message him on the app just to be friendly and see where things went from there. So I set up my own profile – obviously, with a stock image of my own – and I've sent him what I *hope* he'll think is a cute message. Maybe he'll reply."

"Maybe – but you won't be going to meet him without me." Chase's hand squeezed her shoulder. "I hope you know that."

"Veronica!"

The front door flew open, and Sarah blew into the living room, her eyes huge. Immediately, Veronica was on her feet.

"Sarah, what's wrong?" Taking Sarah by the hand, she helped her sit down as Chase hurried forward.

"Look." Pulling out something from her pocket, she handed it to Veronica. Unfolding it, Veronica read it quickly, her heart doing a double flip.

"When did you get this?"

"With tulips. They were delivered to me at my table on my date."

Veronica blinked. "Your date?"

Sarah sniffed as Chase returned with a glass of cold water

and another glass of what looked to be whiskey. "I was out with Justin, remember? Deborah's cousin. The server came over and told me someone had left a bouquet of tulips and a note with them and that they were to be given to me straight away – and obviously, she thought they were from Justin... but I knew they weren't. I had to pretend to him the note was from Deborah."

"That must have been awful for you." Veronica took Sarah's hand as Chase pressed the glass of whiskey into her other hand. "This is getting serious now. Obviously, someone is following you – and watching you."

Sarah closed her eyes. "I wore the green dress to work today. I don't know when he saw me or where, but I'm really scared, Veronica." For a second, it looked like Sarah might collapse back into her chair, her face sheet white, but after a moment, she took in a huge breath and let it out again slowly. "I don't know what to do."

"You're going to stay here with Chase until Deborah and Annie can make it." A sudden urgency ripped through her as she got to her feet. "I have to get to that restaurant."

Sarah's eyes widened. "Why?"

"I need to find out as much as I can about where those tulips came from, and I have to go now. Don't worry, Sarah. You'll be safe here."

"HI THERE." Veronica smiled at the woman behind the counter, who immediately glanced at the screen before her.

"Hi, have you got a reservation?"

"No, but I have a couple of questions if that's okay." Adopting the more business-like manner she used every workday, she kept her smile light as the woman looked back at her in obvious surprise.

"Questions?"

"Yes." Veronica pressed ahead. "There was a woman here on a date this evening. She received an unwanted bouquet of flowers and a note which has scared her, and I am looking into the matter for her."

The woman blinked rapidly. "Oh. I'm sorry to hear that. And are you with the Police Department?"

Veronica shook her head. "I'm afraid I don't have the uniform for it," she quipped, adding a quick smile. "Actually, I'm a private detective." *Where did that come from? Is that what I'm passing myself off as now?*

"I see." The explanation seemed to satisfy her. "I *am* sorry to hear your client is so upset and I'm happy to help you with any questions you have."

"Thank you. I'm very grateful." Pausing for a moment, Veronica collected her thoughts. "I believe it was a bouquet of tulips with an accompanying note. The man asked for them to be delivered immediately and, of course, the server did as was asked."

"Yes, I remember." The woman's smile was a little tight. "I took them from him and then gave them to Melissa to take over."

Veronica's heart skipped a beat. *Maybe she saw the stalker, then.* "Do you remember anything about the man or the flowers?"

"I remember the man who delivered them. He was tall with a warm smile but he did seem in a bit of a hurry – I figured it was because he had a lot of deliveries to make. He was wearing a baseball cap as well, from what I remember."

A question quickly rose in Veronica's mind. "So you think he was from the flower shop?"

She nodded. "Yes, that was my understanding."

"Was there anything about him that could confirm that? Did he have their name on his shirt or anything?"

Hesitating, the woman eventually shook her head. "No,

actually, he didn't. Given his manner and the way he was dressed – not someone who was planning to stop in here for a dinner reservation – I thought that was what he was. The way he spoke to me made it sound like he was just delivering them. He mentioned about it being a busy night and laughed at how he never got a break, especially over the weekend."

So, the stalker could have been here. He could have been only a few steps away from Sarah.

Panic sent adrenaline into Veronica's veins, but reminding herself that Chase was with Sarah, she managed to draw herself back. "Right. And did he mention the flower shop he was from?"

For a few seconds, the woman hesitated. Her gaze ran around the restaurant, her lip caught between her teeth. "Yes, he did. It was just in passing – probably something about them working him so hard – but I'm sure he said he was from 'Vintage Blooms'."

"That place just around the corner?"

The woman nodded. "Yes, that's right."

"Okay, so there's no guarantee this man was actually from 'Vintage Blooms'." Thinking aloud, she saw the woman's eyes flare. "Can I ask if you were here for the rest of evening? Just in case he came in again?"

Her mouth pulled back. "I'm sorry, I'm afraid I went for my break after those flowers arrived." A heavy sigh escaped. "If I'd have known then –"

"You've got nothing to worry about," Veronica reassured her. "Could you give me the description of the man again, please?"

Pulling out her cell, she typed in everything the woman said. She was sure he had dark hair, although most of it had been hidden by a baseball cap, so she couldn't be certain. He had fairly sharp features but a great smile, and she had found him to be very friendly. He had worn a plain t-shirt and jeans, so had been dressed very casually. She hadn't thought anything about that, especially when he mentioned he'd been there to deliver the flowers. Nodding, Veronica jotted it all down.

"You've been very helpful." Smiling, she gestured to her cell. "I'm going to take this back to my friend…I mean, my client. I want to see if she recognizes that description at all."

"I really hope you find him," the woman murmured, passing one hand lightly over her eyes. "I'm so sorry that happened. I just didn't think anything about it."

"And I wouldn't have expected you to. Thank you so much for your help."

"It's been no trouble." The woman reached across the counter and stuck out one hand for Veronica to shake. "And I do hope your friend is okay. In fact, would you wait a moment?"

She ducked behind the counter, writing something Veronica couldn't see, only to then reach across and hand her a card. "And here's a voucher for her. I hope she will come back and that this experience hasn't put her off our restaurant."

"You're very kind." Veronica's heart warmed, her appreciation for the restaurant and its staff growing even higher as she accepted the voucher with a small smile. "I'll give this to her right away. Thank you again for your help."

Heading out of the restaurant, she glanced down at the information the woman had given her. The bouquet had been from 'Vintage Blooms,' which wasn't too far away at all. Anyone who wanted to could easily have bought the bouquet from them and delivered it to the restaurant almost immediately after. She glanced at her watch. It was a little late for the flower shop to still be open, but all the same, Veronica headed toward it, surprised and relieved to meet someone coming out of the door just as she reached it.

"Late night opening?"

The woman looked back at her just as a man came out after her, keys in his hand.

"We had a big order." The woman smiled back at her. "We've got a wedding tomorrow. If there was something you wanted, you could come back tomorrow though?"

"Thank you." Wishing she had a business card she could hand them, Veronica looked from one to the other. "I'm guessing you guys own this place? If it's not too much trouble, I do have a couple of questions I'd like to ask you."

The woman blinked. "About flowers?"

"Uh, no." Sighing, she shook her head. "I don't have any cards or anything made up but that's because I'm just starting out. I'm a private investigator and I have a client with a serious issue that I'm looking into for her."

"Oh, how awful." The woman's eyes widened. "And you think we can help? I'm Susan, by the way. This is Frank." Gesturing to the older man, Veronica made to smile, only for Frank to scowl.

"Who did you say you were again?"

Frank's eyes narrowed a little and Veronica kept her hand by her side instead of sticking it out for him to shake. "I'm Veronica. I'm actually a real estate agent but I work as a private detective on the side." *So the last part isn't exactly accurate but maybe it should be.* "Like I said I have a serious issue with one of my clients and I'm trying to resolve it. If you wouldn't mind giving me a moment or two of your time, I'd be very grateful."

"Oh, sure, of course." Susan seemed to be a good deal more willing to talk to her than Frank. Veronica kept her gaze fixed on Susan rather than glancing at him. "What do you need?"

"My client had a bouquet of tulips delivered to her this

evening, when she was out for dinner at the restaurant around the corner."

"Frank?" The woman glanced to her husband. "You were at the counter this evening."

Still scowling, Frank nodded. "Yes, I remember."

Hope lifted Veronica's heart. "Really?" She tugged her cell out of her pocket and began to read the description of the man she had from the woman at the restaurant. "Was it from this man?"

After a few seconds, the man shrugged his shoulders. "Maybe."

"His eyesight's not the best." Susan clicked her tongue just as Frank muttered and shook his head.

"My eyesight is just fine," he stated firmly. "So yes, it might have been that guy who bought the tulips, although another guy came in soon after and he bought tulips as well."

Veronica's hopes faded. "Just tulips?"

"No, it was part of a bouquet which had had tulips in it." Frank yawned and rubbed one hand over his eyes. "This first guy wasn't in for long. He just picked up a small bouquet, paid for them, and left."

"And how did he pay?"

Frank shrugged. "Cash."

Closing her eyes, Veronica pressed her lips tight together. *I have to find something from this. I* have *to.* "Had you seen him before?" Frustration was making her heart pick up speed. "Had he been in here a couple of weeks ago, perhaps? To make an order of tulips to be delivered?"

Susan sent him a questioning look, but Frank grunted. "No. My eyesight might be bad, but my memory's still sharp."

Veronica bit back her next question, taking in Frank's expression. There were heavy shadows under his eyes, and from his slumped shoulders, she guessed he was tired after a long day and probably desperate just to get on home. Choosing to adopt a sympathetic expression, Veronica offered him a small smile, and for the first time, Frank returned it. "Thank you, Frank. I'll go ahead and tell you what happened." She let her smile fall. "The guy I'm asking you about is bothering my friend. He's been doing it for a while but won't let her know who he is. This evening, she was having a date with someone else and he sent her these tulips just to interrupt her — to freak her out a little."

Susan snatched in a breath. "Really? That's awful!"

"I agree."

"And that's why you're trying to find him?" Frank's eyebrows dropped down low over his eyes. "You're trying to work out who he is so you can help your friend?"

Spreading out her hands, Veronica offered him a wry smile. "It's the only thing I can do."

"Then I wish I could offer you more help." Frank looked at his wife, then shook his head. "The only thing I can say is that he *definitely* came in here but hasn't been in before. That's all I've got for you all."

Stifling a sigh, Veronica nodded. "Thank you. Was there anything about him that caught your attention?"

"No, I'm sorry. Only that he was in a rush." Another shrug lifted his shoulders. "I figured he wanted flowers for a date, but he'd forgotten to buy her something nice." A low chuckle escaped the corner of his mouth. "It happens more than you think. Especially with our flower shop being so close to the major restaurants in this town."

Veronica laughed along with him. "It must be good for business though, right?"

"It's *great* for business." Susan smiled, then leaned back into her husband. "Frank did a good thing here when he put the flower shop where it is. He's built this business from the ground up and done an amazing job of it too."

A soft smile ran across Veronica's face, hearing the love in

Susan's words and seeing Frank's flushed cheeks as he looked away, while at the same time, his arm wrapped around Susan's shoulders.

"I wonder if I might ask you guys to do me a favor? It would be a huge help."

"Oh, sure." Susan nodded immediately, her eyes wide. "Whatever we can do."

"I was hoping you'd take my card. I know it says real estate on it, but like I said, that's my main job. I only do this on the side."

Susan practically snatched it from her fingers. "What is it you want us to do?"

"Simple, really." Veronica stuck her hands in her pockets, elbows akimbo. "If that guy comes in the shop again, would you mind giving me a call? Even better — if you can do it when he's still here."

"So you can come along and see who it is that's been bothering your friend," Frank murmured as Veronica nodded. "That doesn't sound right, what he's doing."

"It's not right," Veronica agreed emphatically, "which is why I was hoping you'd help me find out who he is. He needs to stop doing this to her. She's going through a really difficult time because of him, and I don't like it."

"I don't like it either. I'll give you a call the second he walks back in here again."

"*If* he walks back here again," Frank corrected his wife, although he nodded to Veronica. "We can do that. It's no trouble."

"Thank you. I'm very grateful." With a wave and another word of thanks, Veronica stepped away, moving quickly back towards her car. The sun was already beginning to set, and, for whatever reason, tension crawled up her spine, sending a prickle of nervousness over her skin. There was no reason for her to feel anxious, but telling herself that wasn't stopping her heart from slamming against her ribs. A glance over her shoulder told her no one was following her, but that feeling just kept growing. Unlocking the car, she climbed in quickly but immediately locked the doors, putting her head back and closing her eyes.

I don't know why, but I feel like someone's been watching me.

If it was the same person pursuing Sarah, then maybe she was getting into some really deep trouble. A shudder passed through her as she stuck the key into the ignition and started the car.

Her cell lit up with a notification and a little confused, she swiped at it.

The dating app opened, a little red dot hovering over the messages. Clicking on it, her eyes went to the screen, reading the two lines that *SnakeEyes173* had sent to her.

'You made a good go of it, Veronica, but trying to play pretend won't work with me. I hope Sarah liked the tulips tonight.'

Her eyes swung closed, her heart pounding as fear threaded through her veins. Whoever *SnakeEyes173* was, he had been able to work out exactly who she was and knew what she was trying to do.

I've just been played.

SARAH

*C*rap at her office door had Sarah jumping out of her seat.

I'm way too nervous these days.

When the door swung open, Sarah's stomach dropped. "Mark." It felt like something had wriggled up her spine as Mark walked into her office, looking slightly stony-faced. "Can I help you with something?"

"Yes. I have a client you've worked with previously." His tone was a little stiff. "It would be great if you could give me a couple of tips about how to go about dealing with them. Their case seems a little…frivolous."

"I'd be glad to." *And this is nothing more than a colleague-to-colleague chat. Nothing more.* All the same, her stomach twisted. What if *he* was the person they'd been looking for? What if he was her stalker?

Sarah began, "Okay, so this is Mrs. Pendleton. She is —"

"Before we start, I think we should clear the air." Mark interrupted and came around and sat down opposite her at her desk. His arms folded across his chest, and he lifted one ankle and set it on his knee. Then he pushed his jaw forward.

"Okay." Her heart was beating so quickly that it felt like one beat was running into another. Mark coughed and then glanced at her before pulling his gaze away again. "It's about what I spoke to Caroline about."

Sarah's eyes widened for a second. "Yeah, she did speak to me about that. There's nothing else you need to say, Mark. I took it seriously and want you to feel welcome."

Mark's laugh was a little dry. "Of course, but it's got nothing to do with that. I wanted to talk to you about the gift. I brought you a gift which still you haven't said anything about."

"Right." Was this the moment he'd tell her he'd brought her the tulips? Would he confess that he'd been desperate for her to pay attention to him, to notice him, to fall in love with him? Her skin prickled.

Sighing, Mark looked away. "I overreacted. It's only a cactus."

On hearing this, Sarah's heart immediately began to slow. "You brought me a cactus?" Having very little idea as to where Mark had put the cactus or even when he'd brought it, Sarah felt she had no choice but to play along. "It was very kind of you. Much appreciated. I'm sorry I didn't say that before now." Surreptitiously, she let her gaze run around her office, searching for the aforementioned cactus.

It was nowhere to be seen.

"Okay." Mark left and looked away. "I just didn't know why you haven't said anything."

"The truth is, Mark, I've been struggling with something recently." Deciding to be honest, she spread out her hands. "It's been something really difficult, actually. I'm not saying that's an excuse, but it's a reason."

Mark sighed deeply, shaking his head as if what she'd said wasn't good enough. "I get that, and I think..." Speaking slowly for a second before he continued, he grimaced. "I've gone about this all wrong."

A little confused, she dropped her hands to her sides. "Gone about what?"

"This whole thing." Suddenly a little awkward, Mark rubbed one hand over his hair, shifting his feet a little. "I've heard you're one of the best attorneys here. I have a lot to learn, and I was hoping you might consider mentoring me a little. I never got around to asking that. I wanted to build up to it, so I figured saying hello and bringing a gift might start things off, but...yeah, that was my eventual hope."

Sarah blinked. *I wasn't expecting that.* A little taken aback, she took a few seconds to think about how to respond as Mark shifted his hands, twisting them together, and then let them fall by his sides.

"I really don't know what to say." Still astonished, she let out a quiet laugh. "Honestly, Mark, I don't think you could have said anything else to make me as surprised as I am right now."

His eyes lifted to hers for a second, and then he quickly looked away, his face a little flushed. "I shouldn't have said anything to Caroline about the cactus. That was weird, I know."

"Why did you do that?"

"I don't know." He shrugged. "I guess I was frustrated and, honestly, not thinking clearly. It just came out when she asked me how things were going."

"This place is energy-sapping." *Am I really going to be this sympathetic?*

A wry laugh broke through him. "Things have been tiring at home as well. My newborn isn't sleeping, and I'm trying to take care of my wife as much as possible."

Another wave of surprise crashed against her chest. "You're married?"

A soft smile crossed Mark's face. "Sure am. I have a three-year-old and a three-week-old baby, like I said." His smile fled as he dropped his gaze to the floor. "My wife was so angry with me when she heard what I'd done. It all came out when Caroline talked to me, but I didn't mean it to become this big thing. I'm sorry."

Taking a deep breath, Sarah got out of her chair, walked over, and stuck out one hand. "Then let's start over." There wasn't much to go on, but from what he'd said, Sarah didn't think he could be her stalker. There were other reasons for Mark to have done what he did, and, in her mind, none of those involved stalking her.

It took Mark a second to respond, but when he did, it was with a big smile that split his face. His hand grasped hers.

"I'm so grateful. I really am."

"It's okay. I'm just glad we got all this sorted out. I'm also happy to talk mentoring if that's something you need."

Mark's eyes flared. "Really?"

"Really." She smiled and shrugged. "I'm flattered. How about we set up a meeting for Monday to discuss it in detail?"

A few minutes later, Mark returned to his office, and Sarah slumped back in her office chair, her eyes closing as relief softened her frame.

Looks like I have something to tell Veronica. Mark's not our guy. Her eyes popped open. *And now all I have to do is find that stupid cactus.*

"HI THERE." Sarah opened the door to see Joe's smiling face.

"Hey." He grinned back at her. "I was just delivering your mail when the guy at the bottom of the road said he was delivering this for you. I said I'd take it up to the house since I was coming here anyway."

Sarah's eyes fixed on the parcel Joe held, accompanied by a couple of other letters. *What could it be?*

"Thanks, Joe. I had to call to get it redelivered." She took it from him and looked at the address label, which was printed rather than handwritten. "I definitely didn't order anything, so I have no idea what it is."

"Yeah, but those are the best parcels to get." Joe smiled, turning around, ready to carry on with his rounds. "Hope it's a great surprise."

"Thanks – and thank you for bringing it up here."

"No problem." Walking away, he waved a hand. "I better go. Have a great day."

Smiling to herself, Sarah closed the door and walked back into the living room, setting down the parcel on the small coffee table. The package wasn't very big, so it definitely didn't hold all that much. Peeling back the brown paper, she frowned at seeing a clean white box. It wasn't taped closed, and so she lifted up one edge.

The next second, she pulled back sharply, her breath lodged tight in her chest, a hand squeezing her heart painfully. Her breath came in short, sharp gasps as she leaned forward again, peering into the box.

There were photos of her and James leaving the bar, and her wrapped in his arms just outside of it, and then the two of them getting into a cab. Sitting in the center of the photos, right on top of them all, was one long-stemmed tulip tied with a red ribbon. A white envelope was slotted into the other side, but Sarah couldn't bring herself to open it.

"I need to call Veronica." Speaking to herself, she somehow managed to find her cell and Veronica's number. What she'd said, Sarah couldn't remember, sitting in the quiet house and waiting for her friend to arrive, her eyes still staring at the box.

He sent this to me. He did this deliberately. I'm...I'm scared.

"Sarah?"

With a shriek, Sarah twisted around in her chair only to look into Veronica's eyes. "It's just me. The door wasn't locked, and you weren't answering." Coming closer, she gestured to the box. "This was sent to you?"

Her throat aching, Sarah nodded as Veronica came to sit beside her. "I don't know who would have sent me this." In a hoarse voice, she pointed to the envelope. "There's an envelope too. I haven't opened it."

"Okay." Veronica's steady voice helped her to breathe a little easier. "Are you going to?"

Shaking her head, Sarah looked at her friend. "Can you do it?"

Veronica nodded and made to reach for it, only to pull her hand back. "Just a second." Getting up, she headed to Sarah's kitchen, then came back with a cloth. Using it to pick up the envelope, she carefully lifted it from the box.

"If I were you, Sarah, I would take this straight to the police. I know you haven't told them anything yet, but this is the point where it's necessary. Tell them about what's happened. Give them this envelope. They might be able to get some fingerprints off it."

"I will." Understanding now that the police *had* to get involved, Sarah watched as Veronica used the other end of the cloth to pull the note out from the envelope carefully.

"What does it say?" She couldn't keep the tremble from her voice.

"It only has two words written on it." Veronica's voice had gone very quiet, her eyes fixed on the card.

"What are they?" Her voice was a little more forceful now. Sarah shifted in her seat as her friend held it up. Her world grew very small as she stared at the two handwritten words.

You're mine.

. . .

"AND THAT'S all you can tell me?"

Sarah nodded, a little embarrassed at how much she cried. "Yes." Dropping her gaze to the table, she felt heat climb up her back. "Sorry, I didn't come here before. I figured there wasn't much you could do, so I decided not to bother."

"What matters is that you're here now." The cop smiled at her as Sarah nodded. The cop had been warm but efficient, listening to everything Sarah said and taking notes on everything. She had no doubt the cop understood every aspect of what had happened to her.

"And you say this note was received today?"

Again, Sarah nodded. "As well as the contents of the box."

"Which we have," the cop confirmed. "It was a smart move of your friend picking up the card with a cloth like that. Hopefully, we can get some prints off of it. Although…." Wincing, she shook her head. "In a lot of these cases, the stalkers are clever. They know you might go to the cops, so they make sure to take precautions. But we can be hopeful."

"What should I do while I wait for that?"

The cop offered her another tissue, which Sarah took gratefully.

"It would be wise to be cautious." With a firm look, she rapped lightly on the table. "You're right that you should have come to us before, but now that you have, we can take things from here. Do you have someone you can stay with or who can stay with you? You shouldn't be alone."

"Yes, I do, thanks." Knowing Veronica was outside, waiting for her, and Deborah and Annie, ready to jump in at any moment, helped calm her a little. "I've got good friends, and right now, they're waiting for me."

"Good." The cop smiled. "Try not to overthink this, but do be cautious. And call us if anything changes."

Sarah nodded. "Thanks. I will."

VERONICA

"Hi, I'm looking for Anthony."

The man behind the counter paused, his eyes narrowing slightly. "You're not here for pizza?"

"Oh, no, I'm happy to order pizza as well." Veronica gestured to the menu on the wall. "Give me two of your specials."

The man nodded but still eyed her carefully. "And you say you're looking for Anthony?"

"Sure am." Fixing on a bright smile, she put her hands in her pockets, trying to appear nonchalant. "It's really important I speak to him."

"He's not here." The man's quick response made Veronica tilt her head. It was a little *too* quick. "He's not on shift tonight."

"Yes, he is." Veronica smiled as the man blinked in obvious surprise. "One of your other delivery drivers came out just as I was going in, so I asked about Anthony. He told me Anthony *is* on shift tonight and is around here somewhere. Unless he's gone on a delivery between then and me coming in here — which was all of one minute ago — you really don't need to pretend."

With a roll of his eyes, the man shook his head. "Listen, I don't want any trouble. Anthony's a good delivery driver, but the amount of people who've come in here these last few weeks looking for him is causing me no end of problems."

"Problems?"

The man didn't seem to hear her. "I had three last week, and I've already had one other coming in before you — all realizing that he's been making all these promises he ain't ever going to keep. Anthony's not the sort of guy to want a long-term relationship! He's only in it for the here and now, if you get what I mean."

Veronica's eyes flared. "Wait a second." She spoke slowly, putting her hands down flat on the counter. "Are you trying to tell me Anthony has been seeing more than one woman? And no, I don't mean going out on a date." Her eyes went to his name tag. "You need to tell me the truth, Carter. What's Anthony been up to?"

Carter heaved a sigh, shaking his head. "Just so long as you don't make a scene, okay?" As she nodded, Carter tipped his head a little, his gaze sweeping over her. "You don't seem to be Anthony's usual type, though."

Flushing a little, she fought to keep her expression impassive. "I didn't know he had a type."

"Oh yeah, he does. Usually dark hair or redheads. Like I'm saying, you look a little different from usual, but then again, maybe with everything else he's been up to, it shouldn't surprise me that his tastes have changed."

A heaviness dropped into her stomach, rolling up her throat. "If you could just stick to where Anthony is now, that would be great."

"He's…."

"Carter, another order has come in, it's –"

Veronica didn't recognize the man who had just walked

in from the back of the kitchen, but the way Carter glanced at him and then back to Veronica told her that this guy was who she was looking for.

Gotcha.

"Anthony?" Her chin lifted a notch, arms folded in front of her. "We need to talk."

Immediately, Anthony backed away, his hands lifted. "Listen, I'm sorry. Whatever happened between us, it was only a one-night thing. I thought I'd made that clear and if –"

"We haven't slept together." Clearing her throat, she slung her hands to her hips. "But you *did* go in a date with my friend and I need to talk to you about her."

Anthony blinked, looking to Carter as if he would be able to help him. Anthony was good looking, Veronica thought for herself. The problem was that guys like this made her skin crawl — guys who took advantage of women by pretending they were looking for something more when in fact, they only wanted a one-night stand.

Just as well Sarah's instincts told her to get away from him as quickly as she could.

"If you're here because of your friend, then just tell her I'm sorry." Anthony held out his hands wide. "Like I said, I thought I made it all real clear, but so many of them seem to get it wrong."

"I'm hardly going to believe it's all *their* fault, rather than yours." Veronica rolled her eyes and snorted as Carter let out a little chuckle. "Can I ask why you keep trying to get her attention?"

Anthony blinked. "Who are we talking about, again?"

"Sarah. Sarah Hayes." Watching his expression carefully, Veronica took in the blank expression. Could it be he'd really forgotten about Sarah already? "Maybe because you didn't get what you wanted from her, you thought you'd just keep pushing until she gave in?"

With a shrug, Anthony shook his head. "I'm sorry. I don't know who you're talking about."

"You went on a date with her? It was a couple of months ago."

"He's hardly gonna remember." Carter snorted, ignoring the dirty look Anthony threw back at him. "This guy is out almost every night when he's off shift, going out to dinner or for drinks with a different woman every night. I'm sure he promises them all the same thing, but he doesn't mean a word of it. They'll maybe get a second date if he hasn't managed to get what he wants from them on the first date, but if it's someone who's walked away from him like your friend seems to have done, then I can promise you, Anthony wouldn't have bothered with her any longer. He'll just go find someone else."

"Is that right?" With a lift of her eyebrow, Veronica looked straight back at Anthony, finding herself curling inside with disgust. Guys like this were the worst.

"Let's just stick to the conversation." With a slight cough, Anthony shrugged. "You're asking me if I remember your friend Sarah? Well, I'm sorry, I don't. I don't know who she is, and if we went out on a date that ended badly, then I'm sorry, but I genuinely can't remember her name or face."

There was no reason for Veronica to take him at his word, but given everything Carter had said, she began to suspect this man wasn't the one stalking Sarah. He was obviously quite happy to get what he wanted from anyone he matched with. If Sarah had rejected him, then, from what Carter had said, Anthony wasn't going to get upset about it. He was going to move on.

"Okay." She smiled as Carter. "So let's get my order in. Two of your pizza specials and some garlic bread on the side as well?" Chase would appreciate pizza and garlic bread for dinner, she was sure.

"No problem. This order is on the house." Carter jabbed one finger in Anthony's direction. "And this order is going to come out of your paycheck, Anthony. In fact, this is going to be a new thing. Every time one of these women comes into the shop to look for you, there's going to be consequences. I'm tired of you dragging down the reputation of this pizzeria."

"You can't do that!"

"Yeah, I can. I'm the boss here." Carter shrugged. "Or you could go find another job. It's up to you."

Veronica wasn't exactly sure if this sort of thing was legal, but at the same time, this wasn't her business, and quite frankly, she was a little pleased that Carter was doing something to try and curb Anthony's behavior. Hopefully, that would make him think twice before he took someone else out for dinner.

"Thanks very much."

For the first time, Carter smiled. "That's no problem. I'll get those for you right away."

Two pizzas later, a stack of garlic bread, and a couple of extras that had been given free by Carter, Veronica headed back out to her car with a small smile on her lips. The list of suspects was slowly narrowing, which meant that soon enough, they could work out who was behind all of this.

"I'm going to get you." Muttering to herself, she stuck the key in the ignition, ready to drive home. "You think you can hide behind notes and flowers, but you can't. I'm going to find you."

SARAH

*S*arah paused for a moment, taking in a deep breath.
I can do this.

It had taken some convincing from Veronica for her to still go out on her date with Steve, but after being reminded that it would help take her mind off the situation, she'd decided to go. With a deep breath, she pulled open the door to the bar and stepped inside. To her relief, it wasn't overly loud. The noise from other customers was quiet enough to have a conversation but loud enough not to make things uncomfortable if there was a silence...which there might be, depending on what Steve wanted to say. Surprised when he'd been in touch and even more taken aback when he'd told her he needed to apologize, she'd agreed to go out with him. It wasn't dinner — it wasn't anything more than a quiet drink, just the two of them having a chance to talk.

Her cell buzzed.

Remember, I'm right here.

That brought her a smile. Veronica and Chase were outside somewhere, as were Deborah and Annie. It wasn't as though any of them were worried that Steve might be her stalker after all, but more that they wanted to make sure that anyone else who decided to turn up couldn't escape so easily. After what had happened on her last date with the tulips arriving unexpectedly, Sarah was glad of their company, albeit somewhere outside the bar.

"Sarah?"

Before she knew it, Steve was coming towards her, his expression vastly different than the last time she'd seen him. There was no angry tilt to his jaw, no sparks rampaging through his eyes. Instead, he was calm and quiet, a meekness making him drop his head, his gaze shifting from left to right as if he was too embarrassed to look into her face.

"Hi, Steve." Her hand reached for his, but she quickly pulled it back. This wasn't picking up from where they'd left off, and this *definitely* wasn't a date. Right now, they had a lot of talking to do, and she wasn't about to let herself become caught up with him again before they'd straightened everything out.

"Thank you for coming." He gestured to the table behind him. "Are you okay to sit?"

"Yeah, I'd like that." Following him to the table, aware of her nerves clashing together, she winced hard. They were like bells jangling in her head, overwhelming the noise from the rest of the bar. *I have to keep it together.*

"We have a lot to talk about." Finally, Steve managed to look at her before his eyes dropped away. "And I should start by apologizing."

Sarah nodded slowly. "I would appreciate that." *So long as it's genuine.*

"I should have thought things through. I should have wondered about those messages and why they were being sent to me. I should have listened to you. I should have asked you for an explanation, but instead, I treated you unfairly. I know I hurt you, and I am really sorry." One hand ran over his jaw. "I don't deserve to have you sitting here like this with me. You'd be well within your rights to say that, after what I did and said, you could never let me back into your life. But instead, you decided to give me another shot and I'm grateful for that."

"I appreciate everything you said, Steve. I'm not going to pretend I wasn't hurt by what you did or what you said. I was." She offered him a small smile. "But at the same time, I can understand it. Things have been so weird for me recently, there's no reason why you would know about it, mostly because I didn't tell you."

"*Why* didn't you tell me?"

She shrugged. "Because we'd only had three dates." It was her only explanation and, thankfully, Steve seemed to know what she meant, given the way he smiled.

"I wouldn't have run away if that's what you were worried about."

"That was *exactly* what I was worried about." With a timid smile, she looked away from him. "I mean, it sounds almost impossible to believe, doesn't it? Someone is after me, confusing me and upsetting me for no explicable reason – and I can't figure out who it is."

Steve nodded slowly. "Can you tell me exactly what's been going on? I'd like to hear it from the beginning if you'd be willing to share it?" His mouth twisted. "I should have said this much sooner. I'm sorry."

"It's okay. Like I said, I get it." Taking a deep breath and starting from the beginning, she told him about the flowers and the one she'd found in the morning. She told him about the bouquet of tulips, which had come later, that she'd assumed had been from him. She told him how she found one on her doorstep with a red ribbon, and about the note she'd gotten at work. Not missing a single thing, Sarah told him everything, and as he listened, Steve's face grew dark with obvious anger. It was anger she appreciated, in a way. She didn't have to ask whether or not he believed her. It was clear enough.

"I'm *so* sorry, Sarah." Steve gripped her hand, his jaw working as he pushed out a long breath through gritted teeth. "I should have believed you from the beginning. I'm sorry I didn't." Blinking, he looked away. "And you have no idea who this is or why they want to get your attention like this?"

"I've got no idea." Sarah put her other hand on top of their joined ones, finding she appreciated the comfort that came from his touch. "If I could figure out who they were, I'd be able to put an end to all of this."

Steve's eyebrows lifted high. "Why? What do you think would happen?"

"I... I don't know. Maybe if I talked to whoever this is, made it clear that I'm not interested?"

Scowling, Steve's fingers squeezed a little tighter on hers. "I don't think someone like this is up for chatting, Sarah. Whoever this guy is, he wants you in an unhealthy and twisted way. Talking to him won't do any good. From what I know – and I'll admit, I don't know much – guys like this are obsessed. Even if you told him you weren't interested, in his mind, you're already together. You could really be in danger. You've got to take this seriously."

Something dark grew like a cloud over her head, and she shuddered, clinging now to Steve's hand. "I *am* taking it seriously, Steve. Veronica's helping me to get to the bottom of all this, and I've talked to the cops." *Only after a lot of encouragement, I'll admit.* "I've even got my friends sitting outside this place right now."

His eyebrows shot up, and he glanced at the window. "Really?"

"Really."

Relief pulled at his expression. "That's good to know. You've got good friends, Sarah."

She smiled. "Yes, I absolutely do."

Her lips pressed hard together as his hand went to her shoulder, and for the first time that evening, tears began to burn behind her eyes.

"Let me go get us something to drink."

Dabbing at her eyes, Sarah sniffed hard as Steve headed to the bar. He was being so kind and was clearly concerned for her. It was apparent he regretted how he'd behaved before, and while she was grateful for that, just being here with him again brought her so much comfort. She could trust and rely on him, and that meant the world to her.

"Glass of white wine." He set it down in front of her and took his seat. "I hope that's okay."

"It's great." Her heart lurched at the softness of his smile. "I know this has been really weird, but I am grateful to you for being here with me. If you're willing to try dating me again, despite this crazy stalker I've got, then I'd love to go out again."

To her surprise, Steve shook his head only to give her a rueful laugh. "I can't believe you're saying that to me. I should be saying all that to *you*." When she smiled, he took her hand again. "I really like you, Sarah. I hated it when I got those messages. I reacted badly, but it was like someone had gone into my chest and ripped my heart out. Maybe it's a little too soon to be saying all that, but the truth is I really like you... and I'm desperate for a second chance."

"I feel the same." Speaking quietly, Sarah tilted her head, a grin spreading across her face. "Want to know something? I went out on another date."

For a second Steve didn't respond and then, when he did, it was only with a rough clearing of his throat as he shifted in his chair, his hand letting go of hers.

"After you ended things, my friend set me up with her cousin." Still smiling, Sarah let out a quiet laugh at his dark frown. "He was *great*."

"You're really going to try and make me suffer, aren't you."

"Don't see why not." Laughing, she reached out to touch his arm, seeing the sparks flashing in his eyes. "But that's not why I'm telling you all this. I wanted to share that I was on a date with Justin; while he was a great guy, and I enjoyed spending time with him, he was nothing compared to you. You called me when I was sitting down at the table with him, and despite the fact things weren't good between us, you were the only thing I could think about. I kept wishing *you* were the one I was sitting on the table with, not him."

Steve's eyes closed for a second, and then he smiled. "Really?" Surprise dotted across his face as she squeezed his arm. "I think you might have caught me. Steve."

"I feel the same about you."

She leaned closer, wondering if this was the moment when they might share a kiss. Her cell phone buzzed. With a groan, she looked down at it, only for an unfamiliar number to pop up on the screen. A message followed.

Her breath hitched.

"Wait." Steve glanced at her cell, then frowned. "Are you telling me that number is messaging you? I thought you changed your number."

"I did." Sarah's heart began to flood in panic. "I don't remember the number from the last time they called me – but look what they sent me." She picked up her cell with a trembling hand and handed it to him, the words already etched into her memory.

I pushed him away once. I can push him away again. The only person for you is me.

138

Grimacing, Steve glanced around the bar. "He's here. He's *got* to be here, watching us."

"I don't understand. I don't know how this happened. I've already changed my number. How could he have gotten my new one?"

"I don't know, but I think you should stay somewhere else tonight," Steve said gently, but his gaze was firm. "It's not safe for you to be alone. Is there somewhere you can go? I'd be more than happy to let you stay with me, but I don't want you to think that's the only thing I've got on my mind - I don't. The only thing I want is for you to be safe."

Saying nothing, Sarah passed one hand over her eyes. Fear was drumming through her with every heartbeat, making it hard to think clearly.

"Sarah?"

"I was determined to show him I wouldn't let him get in my way. I was going to ignore him and carry on with my life. I tried that with Justin, and I'm scared he will escalate to something worse." Her throat constricted, and she let out a half sob, closing her eyes tight. "It was dumb to think I could escape him — that showing him a bit of strength would make him stop."

Steve's hand closed over hers, but its strength was reassuring, softening her fears bit by bit. "You *are* strong. That's what you are, Sarah. You are brave. You are tough. You've dealt with so much already by yourself, but this needs more than just you and your friends. We need to go to the cops."

Sniffing, she blinked quickly to keep the tears back. "I filed a report yesterday, but that's all they can do. A note had arrived for me, but I'm guessing there hasn't been anything on that since they haven't called me about it."

"Then you need to stay somewhere tonight. You can't be alone."

Sarah didn't know what it was, but there was something

about Steve – whether it was his solid presence or strength – she couldn't think of anyone better than him. "Can I stay with you?

He didn't even hesitate. "Of course, you can. But I want you to call your friends and let them know that's what you're doing. Someone needs to know where you are, and I want you to be able to trust me."

She smiled with a flood of relief as she looked into his eyes. "You're a good man, Steve."

He gave her hand a reassuring squeeze. "I'll do anything for you, Sarah."

He was all she needed right now, her anchor as the storm raged around her. She trusted he wouldn't let her go.

"Veronica?"

"Hey, are you okay?" Her voice was filled with concern, but Sarah managed to smile. "I'm absolutely fine. I'm with Steve. Something… something happened, but I'm all right."

"What happened?"

Taking a deep breath, Sarah let it out slowly, aware of how it trembled. "I got a message."

There was a beat of silence. "From *him*?"

"Yeah, from him. I already changed my number, so I don't know how he got it."

"Oh no." A heavy sigh sounded through the phone. "I'm sorry, Sarah. I feel like I'm letting you down."

"No, you're not. You got me to go to the cops, which was more than I think I'd have done on my own. *And* you've narrowed the list down. How many people have we got left?"

There came a long silence. Frowning, Sarah plucked nervously at the napkin, her heart turning over as if it knew something significant was coming.

"There's no one."

Sarah caught her breath. "What?"

"I visited the pizza place earlier this evening, and I'm sure it's not Anthony."

"And it's not Danny," Sarah continued slowly. "It's not Steve. And you already told me about Phillip."

"Yep. His wedding isn't too long from now."

"Then who's left? Mark?"

"You said yourself that —"

"Jake?"

There was a breath of hesitation. "It could be, but that wouldn't make much sense."

A swell of desperation broke through her, and Sarah stifled a cry of frustration and fear. "How am I supposed to find out who's stalking me if there's no one left on the list?"

"I don't know," Veronica answered quietly. "But I'm still working on this. I won't give up."

Steve patted her hand, aware she was upset, and she managed a shaky smile in return.

"I — I'm going to go stay with Steve tonight. I know you offered, but so has he. And maybe... maybe this will surprise my stalker. Maybe he won't expect me to be staying with him."

"Okay." There was heaviness to Veronica's voice, which hadn't been there before. "You do what you think is best."

"Steve's not my stalker." Speaking with determination, Sarah immediately closed her eyes.

"Absolutely, he's not," Veronica agreed. "I just want you to be careful. My preference would be you go to the cops, tell them what's happened and that you need extra protection, but —"

"I'll be okay." Interrupting Veronica, Sarah spoke with more confidence than she felt. "I've *got* to be okay."

VERONICA

"*L*et me look at this again."

Going home wasn't what Veronica wanted, but there was no reason to stay out, not when Steve had already taken Sarah back to his place. Deborah and Annie had headed home too, clearly still worried about their friend but seeing there wasn't much else to do.

"How are you feeling?" Chase wandered into the living room, following his question with a yawn. It was already late, and they were both tired, but Veronica couldn't sleep. Something about this whole thing was bothering her, and no matter how she tried, she couldn't get the situation out of her head.

"I'm frustrated. I'm definitely missing something."

"I don't think you are." Chase put a comforting hand on her shoulder as she rubbed her forehead. "I think you've listed everyone and everything."

"But it doesn't make sense." With one hand balled tight in frustration, she looked down at the list again in the hope that the words might give her a clue she'd not seen before. "I must be missing someone. Someone obvious."

"Well, who do you have?"

Sitting down at the table, Chase clutched his coffee mug. Sure, it was late, but he was obviously able to tell she wouldn't be able to sleep. "Start from the beginning."

"Anthony: not interested in a long-term relationship and has been out with so many women he can't even remember who Sarah is."

"Unless he's pretending? Faking it just to escape your questions?"

Veronica grimaced. "I don't think he was. The guy couldn't keep his reactions hidden, and his expression just screamed that he wanted to get out of there. He couldn't hide what he was feeling from me even if he wanted to."

"So we move onto Danny."

She sighed. "It could be him but he made himself so obvious it doesn't seem like it." Rubbing one hand over her eyes and aware of the fatigue pulling at her, she shook her head. "If he *was* her stalker, then leaving that note on her car was an idiotic thing to do. Especially since he signed it."

Chase nodded. "Okay. So next there's…?"

"Mark, and again, my gut says no. He went on about the gift Sarah didn't thank him for, but they got that straightened out. *Plus*, he's married with one kid and a newborn, which explains the bad mood."

"But he *could* get her number," Chase reasoned. "He could get it from HR."

"Yes, but then he'd have to explain why he needed her personal cell number from them instead of just asking her for it, and I'm sure someone would have told Sarah if he had done that."

With a sigh, Chase sat down at the table next to her. "Then our list is narrowing."

"It sure is." She shook her head. "We haven't put Steve on

the list, but I don't think it's him. Which leaves us with Jake, but like I said, I don't think it's him either."

"Which means that someone else, as in someone else *entirely*."

"Yeah, I think so too. Someone neither Sarah nor I have thought about yet."

Chase put one hand over his eyes. "That doesn't help. There's bound to be a ton of guys in her life, some of whom she barely knows. How can you possibly narrow it down?"

Veronica tapped her pen on her notebook. "It's got to be someone she sees fairly regularly, someone who can get her cell number."

"Okay, so how about we come up with ways that people can get your cell number."

Nodding at Chase's suggestion, Veronica began to write. Ideas flew between them, and she wrote everyone down.

"Wait." A sudden thought had her eyes fixed on the paper, her heart throwing itself back into her chest. "There's one we haven't thought of yet." Writing it down, she pushed it towards Chase and saw his eyes flare. Then, the color slowly drained from his face. "Veronica." Hoarseness tightened his voice, and Veronica nodded wordlessly, staring at the paper and realizing she might have hit on the truth.

I'm terrified about what this might mean for Sarah.

"I can't know for sure." Finding his hand, she gripped it tightly. "I can't say anything, really. Not until I've asked Sarah a couple of questions."

"But it all makes sense if you think about it." Chase's hand tightened on hers. "If it's no one else, then it's gotta be him."

The tension in her chest grew sharply, and Veronica's heart began to hammer as she looked at her cell, wondering if she could call Sarah now.

"I don't think it will matter if you wake her." Seeming to

know her thoughts, Chase offered her a small smile, which faded quickly. "Go call her. I'll grab us some more coffee."

As Veronica dialed Sarah's number and held the cell to her ear, all she could picture was Sarah being confronted by her stalker. Veronica's eyes squeezed closed, hopeful and yet half terrified of what Sarah's answers could mean. She let out a slow breath. Either this was exactly who they'd been searching for, or she'd be back to staring at the blank page again.

SARAH

*S*arah looked up into the darkness and smiled softly. Things with Steve had gone well, and her fears slowly faded. When they'd arrived at his place, he'd shown her around so she'd know where everything was. His house was really secure, with locked windows and doors and an intruder alarm. When he'd offered her the choice of bedrooms, she'd taken the one at the top of the stairs, complete with an en suite.

Steve is such a great guy.

Her smile grew. Steve hadn't made any sort of advances, obviously aware it wasn't the right time, but all the same, her heart had filled with a gentle affection for him. Steve was an amazing guy, and once all this was behind her, she was determined to take things forward with him.

Her cell buzzed, and Sarah jumped, startled by the sound. Instantly, the memory of her last message coming through sent a jolt of fear through her, and she closed her eyes, shuddering slightly. When it buzzed again, Sarah grabbed it and turned it off completely, not even glancing at the screen. She didn't want to hear anything more from her stalker, and that meant not even looking at her cell phone.

I should have turned it off the minute I got here.

There was no need for her to leave it on. Veronica knew where she was, and right now, the best thing she could do for herself was have a good sleep. Turning over to her side, she snuggled down into the pillow. After a difficult evening, she was finally a little more at ease. Steve was here and she was safe, which meant all she had to do now was go to sleep.

SOMETHING HAD WOKEN HER. A little frustrated, Sarah huddled back into the warmth of the blanket, trying to close her eyes and return to the dreamless sleep she so desperately needed.

A warning began to jangle through her mind.

I'm just on edge after everything that happened.

All the same, sleep seemed more and more distant, and with a heavy sigh, Sarah sat up and swung her feet flat on the floor. Sitting up straight, she groaned again and pinched the bridge of her nose to try and wake up.

Maybe a glass of water would help.

A familiar scent filled the air, and Sarah frowned. It was unpleasant and it made her insides curl with fear.

That's smoke.

Her heart climbed up to her throat as she got to her feet and hit the light, seeing the first few wisps of smoke drifting through the bottom of the door.

I've got to get out of here!

Looking around wildly, she tried to corral her thoughts. She grabbed an old hoodie she'd picked up from home on her way over to Steve's place and threw it over her head. Pulling the hood over her head, she slung on her sneakers and got to her feet again.

"Sarah!"

Before she could answer, the door pushed open, and Steve stepped through it, slamming it closed and leaning back against it as if by doing so, he could keep the smoke behind him.

"Sarah, there's a fire, and we need to move. I don't know where it started, but it's seeping smoke through the whole house. I've called the fire station, and they're on their way, but we have to go. Now."

The wail of a fire engine sounded as she clasped his hand tightly. Pulling her hoodie closer over her head, she tucked her hand back into her sleeve and then pressed the sleeve to her mouth, trying to breathe through it. When Steve opened the door, the wall of smoke poured over them. Steve stepped forward, moving quickly, and Sarah followed. He cautiously began to descend the stairs, Sarah following on wobbly legs.

The dark smoke was everywhere, shrouding everything in shadow. It was already nighttime, which meant there was barely any light, and walking through the house felt like she was walking through night itself. Her eyes were burning as she tried not to cough or even breathe. Heat was everywhere. She could feel it on her skin. Fear began to grab a hold of her, but the next second, somebody was shouting. There was a sudden sound — a slam, a crash, and a sudden clearing of the air. Steve rushed forward and she went with him, staggering outside as one of the firefighters grasped her arm, leading her toward safety.

"What happened?" One of the firefighters ran towards them, giving them both a bottle of water. "Is there anyone else in the house?"

Wrapping one arm around Sarah, Steve pulled her close, and she rested her head on his chest, utterly worn out. "No. It was just the two of us."

Steve answered most of their questions, and Sarah leaned

even more into him, her eyes closing. She was safe. Steve was safe, and whoever had done this wouldn't dare come scuttling out now. The firefighters were here. The cops would be on their way.

"You both need to get checked over by the EMTs." The firefighter gestured for them to retreat further from the house.

"Thanks," Sarah tried to say, only to be interrupted by a fit of coughing. The firefighter jerked his thumb toward the ambulance and then moved to the house.

"They think the fire is in the basement," Steve told her, one arm around her shoulders. "That's why all the smoke took so long to rise. I didn't know where it was coming from, but hopefully, there won't be too much damage." He looked down at her, pausing for a moment. "I'm glad you're safe. Are you okay?"

"I'm fine." Closing her eyes, she let herself shiver. "I can't imagine what they've done to your house."

"We don't know for sure how the fire started, but none of that matters to me." The zeal in Steve's voice made her believe him. "I wanted to keep you safe. I want you to feel like you're safe with me. I can't imagine what he might have done if you'd been home alone."

I don't even want to think about that.

Shuddering, she closed her eyes for a second. "Thank you, Steve." Trying to keep her fear from overwhelming her, she turned to look at him, stopping in the middle of the sidewalk. "This is because of me, Steve. I'm so sorry."

He gripped her hand hard. "This is *nothing* to do with you."

"But my stalker did this, I'm sure." Her throat closed up, her words piling on top of each other until she could barely get a single one out. "By staying here with you, I brought him here."

Steve pulled her close. "You don't know that," he answered firmly. "But even if it is, that doesn't mean you're to blame. I wouldn't have asked you here if I didn't accept that there might be risks — and believe me, Sarah, you're worth the risk."

When he dropped his head to kiss her, Sarah was ready, letting his arms sling around her waist as she pulled herself close. It was brief, but it was enough.

"I'm here for you." Smiling softly, he turned and led her towards the ambulance. "Always."

VERONICA

"*S*he still not picking up." Veronica began to pace across the living room floor, Chase watching her. "I'm sure I'm right. I'm *sure* I'm right, but I have to ask her some questions to know for sure."

"Most likely, she's asleep." Chase lifted both shoulders. "I know you keep calling, and it goes straight to voicemail, but there *is* a chance she might just be asleep. She's turned her cell off so she can get a few hours of uninterrupted rest. That's what she needs right now."

"Yes, I know that." A flame of guilt licked up through her. "But this is more important. It's not like her cell to go straight to voicemail like that. I'm sure there's something wrong. I'm worried for her."

"There is another possibility, you know." A slow smile began to spread across his face as Veronica frowned, looking at him. "Come on, Veronica, I thought you were meant to be a sleuth!"

Letting out an exasperated breath, she threw up her hands. "Thought of what?"

"The fact that she's at Steve's place." Wiggling his

eyebrows, Chase chuckled as she rolled her eyes. "They've been out on a few dates, and this is them reconciling. Don't you think there's a chance that —"

"Maybe." Not wanting to go into any further detail, she sighed heavily and shook her head. "Okay, so that probably is the most obvious answer, and yes, I shouldn't be going crazy and worrying about her and calling her like that all the time, but I can't help it. I'm *really* worried."

"I get you are, but if she's with Steve, then she's going to be just fine."

"Unless the stalker has been watching her," Veronica reminded him, her worries still lingering. "Don't forget, the message he sent her tonight was one saying that he'd pushed Steve away before, and he was going to push him away again. If he hadn't been watching her at the bar, then how would he know they were together?"

"You're right." Chase frowned and ran one hand through his hair. "She should have gone to the cops."

"She didn't want to – and she does have Steve, but all the same, I'm still worried. Like I said, it's not like her to turn off her cell, but maybe if she's with Steve, then you're right. That's the reason she's done it."

With a nod, Chase opened his mouth to say something else, only to be interrupted by her cell phone ringing. Grabbing it, Veronica answered it before she could even see who was calling. "Sarah? Is that you?"

"It's Annie." There was an edge to her voice that had Veronica stopping dead, freezing in place. "I just heard there's been a fire. I'm at home, but I asked one of my colleagues to let me know if anything came in tonight, just as a favor. She called me a few minutes ago with this."

"A fire?" Blinking, Veronica swallowed hard. "Where?"

"The same street as Steve's house." Annie's quiet voice

held all of the same concern that was growing in Veronica's heart. "Do you think he's….?"

"I don't think Steve's the stalker, no." Chase had come over to her, and grasping his hand, she leaned into him. "But I do think that the stalker could have set a fire at Steve's place." *Why didn't I force her to go to the cops?* "Maybe he followed her back there."

"There's already plenty of EMTs on the scene," Annie said quickly, "but I'm going over there myself."

"We'll join you." Seeing Chase nod, she squeezed his hand. "And I'll call Deborah on the way."

"Thanks. I'll see you there."

Ending the call, Veronica went to grab her keys, with Chase already at the door. "Chase, I think the stalker set a fire at Steve's place."

He said nothing, holding the door open for her.

"I think…" Her heart was beating so fast that it hurt. "I think there's a chance he's trying to force Sarah away from Steve."

"Or hurt Steve?"

With a tight nod, she hurried out past him as Chase closed the door behind them both. "Or so he can grab her." The words burned on her lips, but she forced herself to say them. "That's always a possibility."

Chase sprinted to the car alongside her. "Grab her?" he repeated, his breathing a little fast now. "But why?"

"Because he's been escalating things." Her gut twisted as she got into the car. "This is the last stage, isn't it? Instead of messaging her, sending her flowers, and staying in the background, he's got to step forward. He's got to take her away so he can fit her into whatever fantasy he's built for himself." Nausea rolled in her stomach. "It's just a matter of time, Chase. We have to get to her before it's too late."

. . .

BY THE TIME they got to Steve's place, there was nothing but smoke and a few fire trucks, their lights flashing along the rest of the street. Having parked the car, Veronica and Chase hurried towards the house.

"Sorry." A broad-shouldered cop held out one hand. "This needs to be kept clear right now."

"We're here for our friend," Veronica spoke urgently. "Sarah? Sarah Hayes? She was staying in the house. I've been trying to get a hold of her, and I can't."

"Maybe she left her cell in the house." His expression softened, obviously taking in Veronica's terrified expression. "Okay, on you go. The last place I saw her was over at the ambulance with the EMTs and her boyfriend. Samuel, was it?"

"Steve," Chase corrected, but Veronica had already gone. Hurrying towards the ambulance, she searched frantically for her friend.

She's not here.

Shifting to the ambulance itself, she spotted a familiar face.

"Steve!" She saw him sitting at the back of the ambulance. His arm was extended with a blood pressure cuff on it, and it looked like he had an oxygen mask over his face. She rushed forward. "Steve, are you okay?"

Wearily, he looked up at her, his eyes appearing sunken as he plucked the mask off his face. "Veronica. Hi."

"Steve." Chase hurried towards them both. "You're hurt?"

"I'm fine." Gesturing to the paramedic, he managed a wry smile. "They're just making sure my lungs are okay. I have a bit of asthma, so inhaling the smoke was a real bad idea." At a sharp look from the paramedic, he dropped the mask back in place.

"I'm glad you're okay." Taking a moment, Veronica tried to calm her rising panic. "Where's Sarah?"

Steve waved one hand, then plucked off his mask again. "She's shaken but she's okay. I think she's worried that…well, you know."

Veronica nodded. "Where is she?"

"She went to get us both another bottle of water."

Slumping a little with relief, Veronica rubbed at her eyes, with Chase putting one arm around her shoulders. "Then she's okay."

"Yes, she's fine," Steve confirmed. "She's blaming herself, but I'm telling her that none of this is her fault. It's not like she *asked* that guy – whoever he is – to do this. She didn't demand he set a fire in my basement."

"And why do you think he did that?"

In answer to Chase's question, Steve shrugged. "To get back at me since I'm getting close to Sarah, and he's not?"

"That might be it," Veronica agreed quickly. "Or he might find a way to drive you both out of the house. After all, it's not like he soaked the floors with kerosene and then set fire to it. He just made something which would give enough smoke to have you both out of the house." The relief she'd felt for only a few moments faded completely, leaving her worries to build again. "She's taking an awful long time to get those bottles of water."

"Yes, she is." Again, Steve lifted the mask, but the paramedic gestured to him, and he snapped it back on his face again.

"I'll go look for her," Chase murmured as Veronica nodded.

Swallowing at the ache in her throat, she scanned the area. "I'll go this way," she pointed. "You go that way."

With a wave to Steve, she turned and hurried into the gloom, searching for her friend. The street was lit by only a few dull streetlights, and aside from the ambulances, fire trucks, and a couple of cop cars, there was nothing else. A few civilian cars were dotted around the place, but at this point, she had no idea where Sarah might have gone. If she hadn't gone to get the water bottles, then where would she be?

Is he here?

The dark thought pierced Veronica, and she pressed one hand to her stomach, sucking in air repeatedly. There was no movement, no crying for help, no sudden exclamation. *Maybe I'm being overreacting. Maybe she's just fine. Maybe —*

Her thoughts were cut by the sound of a car door slamming. Had she heard a shriek, or did she just imagine it? Rushing forward, she ran out into the road, rounding a corner just in time to see someone dragging Sarah to a car. She was crying out, but the man had pressed something to her nose and mouth, and after a few seconds, Sarah slumped into his arms, and he began to shove her into his car.

"Stop!" Veronica began to run, her heart pounding. The lights were so dim she couldn't see who the guy was, but she had no doubt over what she'd just seen. The guy sprinted around to the driver's side, got in, and revved the engine.

He pulled away from the curb and drove straight at her.

Sarah. I can't leave her, I –

All Veronica could see were bright lights, her whole body immobilized. She couldn't seem to move or shift one way or the other. Death was coming, and she couldn't get out of its way.

"Veronica!"

A scream lodged in her throat as strong arms wrapped around her, yanking her to one side as they fell heavily to the blacktop.

"Veronica." Chase was breathing hard, and his arm was still wrapped protectively around her as he fought to sit up. "Are you okay?"

"I saw Sarah." Struggling to get the words out, she made

to sit up, but dizziness overwhelmed her. Leaning back against Chase, she took a few seconds to try and recover. "I saw him, Chase." Tears pricked at the edges of her eyes. "I'm sure I saw him."

"Okay." Chase helped her sit up, then shifted to sit by her on the side of the road. "Who is it then? You need to tell the cops and tell him your suspicions."

"I know." A fresh pain pierced her. "Sarah was with him. He was pulling her. She was... she was calling for me. And then he put something to her nose and mouth, and she was gone."

"You're going to be able to help her." Chase's firm tone helped bolster her slightly. "Don't start thinking you can't do anything – or haven't done anything. You absolutely have, and Sarah was calling for you because she knew that you could help - that's what you're going to do. You're going to find her, and you're going to bring her back here safely."

I can't start losing myself in regret now. I have to fight for her. I have to find her. "You're right. I can't give up – and I'm going to need Annie's help."

SARAH

"*And* before you ask, no, there's no point in screaming. No one can hear you."

Sarah's stomach clamped hard as she slowly looked around her. Her vision was blurry, her muscles aching, and as she reached to rub at her eyes, she realized her hands were cable-tied.

He'd taken her.

A scream lodged itself in her throat but she didn't let it free. He was right. No one could hear her, but she had to hope Veronica had seen her before he'd put that cloth over her face and knocked her senses right out of her.

"Tell me you understand."

Shivering, she closed her eyes tight. "I understand." The voice that came out of her wasn't one she recognized.

A chuckle emerged from the dark beside her. She recoiled at the sound.

"I hope you see the truth now, Sarah. It's always been you and me."

Another shiver ran through her as she tried to shift in the seat. She'd been surprised to see him at the fire, but figuring most people in town would have heard of it by now, she'd gone to speak to him. When he'd expressed concern, she smiled and put her hand on his arm, and he'd pulled her into a hug... and then dragged her to his car. Nobody had heard her screaming. He'd clamped one hand over her mouth, blocking out the sound as best he could, but had been forced to lift it when he opened the car door. He'd been stronger than she'd expected. She was already weakened from the fire. Her brief hope had been the glimpse of Veronica, and she'd managed to cry out one more time before he'd put something over her nose and mouth.

That was the last thing she remembered. Now she was here with him. Trapped. Dread pooled in her stomach, chilling her from head to toe as she shivered again. "I — I'm sorry. I didn't realize you felt this way about me."

Swiveling in his seat, he turned, his eyes blazing with a sudden anger. "Don't you *dare* lie to me. I've spent *months* telling you, showing you how I felt and you've ignored every single thing."

"I didn't ignore you. I swear." Her heart was hammering so hard it was difficult to get her breath. "I didn't know. I promise you. I didn't know."

"Stop lying!" The slap that hit her across the face sent her head slamming into the side of the car, pain ricocheting through her. "You're going to have to learn what happens to you when you lie. I *won't* have a wife who lies to me."

Wife?

Her ears still ringing, her head aching, Sarah fell silent. There was nothing she dared say.

"I'm going to go and get things ready for us, and you're going to stay right here in the garage. Maybe think about what you're going to say to me when I return."

Her eyes squeezed closed again as he got out of the car. The next second, the sounds of scraping rattled through to her, and she couldn't help but look. For whatever reason, he was shoving something towards her side of the car. It took him a lot of strength, a lot of pushing and grunting, but eventually, a huge metal filing cabinet was pressed hard against her car door, blocking hers and the driver's side door. His grin made her twist her head away. The darkness of it petrified her.

"Wouldn't want you setting off the car alarm and alerting all the neighbors now, would we?" With a rap of his knuckles on the car, he walked away towards the house door house, slamming it shut behind him. She shuddered violently before shoving off the blanket he'd put over her – not to keep her warm but to keep her hidden.

I have to get out.

That was her only thought. She tried the car door but soon realized the huge filing cabinet he'd pushed in front of it wouldn't let her out. It had completely blocked her door and his. Even if she tried to go that way, she couldn't, and he was parked too close to the wall on the other side to give her any space to get out that way. For the moment, she was trapped.

Slamming herself back in her seat, tears began to burn as sobs pulled at her chest.

How did I miss this?

He'd always been there on the fringes of her life, fading in and out. They weren't friends, but obviously, to him, they were something more, something he'd wanted for a long time...and something she'd never seen in him before.

And now he's caught me. What's he going to do to me?

The unspoken fear that she was about to die rattled through her, and shuddering, she put her bound hands to her face, trying to find even a tiny breath of calm.

For a second, hope flared as she scrabbled around, her arms twisting painfully as she checked for her cell phone.

That hope died as she remembered she'd left it behind when she ran from the fire. No doubt he'd been counting on that, and even if she'd had the presence of mind to take it, no doubt he'd have made sure it was thrown away on their drive here. She closed her eyes again and pressed her hands to her cheeks, trying to hold back the tears. She didn't know how he'd react if he saw her crying. Her instinct told her he wanted her happy, glad, in fact, that he'd finally found her, *claimed* her even. That was what the fire had been for, she realized. It hadn't been meant to hurt her *or* Steve. Steve hadn't even really been a part of it. The only thing he wanted to use the fire for was as a cover to pull her away. She ought to have been much more cautious and guarded, but seeing a friendly face after everything that had happened had been a comfort. She'd never expected he'd be the one to strike out at her. He'd never even been a consideration.

A single tear ran down her cheek as a sudden realization hit her full force.

He said he was taking a page out of my book using the dating app...but I never told him I was using an app.

Another tremble shook her violently, her skin covered in goosebumps. *And he took my parcel from the delivery guy – and my cell number would have been on the paperwork somewhere, just in case it got lost or something. He could have gotten my new cell that way.* Dropping her head forward, her chin to her chest, she stifled another sob. *With delivering the letters every day, he could have watched me through the window or watched me leave for work. That's how he knew I was in a green dress.*

The man she'd never thought about, the man she'd never even *dreamt* of imagining...*he* was her stalker. A friendly face turned into her nightmare.

Joe.

Even Steve's number wouldn't have been all that difficult to find, not for someone like Joe. He could have gone to the site where Steve was working and asked for some details, claiming a delivery needed a cell number. It was all so clear to her now and yet, at the same time, utterly terrifying.

I have to try and think clearly.

Taking in as slow a breath as she could and refusing to let panic settle in and steal away her senses, Sarah dropped her hands to her lap and shook her head, trying to clear her thoughts. If he took her inside, she probably wouldn't come back out again unless Veronica or the cops worked out where she was – and by then, it would probably be too late. That was difficult to accept, but she took a deep breath to steady herself.

So I need to escape.

Instinct told her it was going to be futile. There wasn't any way to get out. All the doors were blocked, making her a prisoner while still giving her the freedom to move about in the car. Trying one of the car doors, she could open it a little but nowhere near enough to get out. Her blood began to pound in her ears as she fought through the panic, trying to think of another way to save herself.

Perhaps I don't have to escape at all.

"The cops will be looking for me by now. Veronica will be, too." Speaking out loud, she tried uselessly to break apart the cable tie that rubbed hard at her wrists, wincing with the pain and then slumping back into her seat when it didn't break.

Okay, so I can't get out. I can't get free of this. So maybe I need to buy myself as much time as I can.

A sudden noise made her jump, her heart freezing in her throat. When Joe didn't appear, she let herself breathe more easily and then shifted to the front of the car, peering out of the windshield to see more of the garage. A single bulb hung from the ceiling, pushing shadows everywhere; shadows that reached out for her, lurching towards her, telling her that she would never escape.

Swallowing at the ache in her throat, she closed her eyes. The only thing she could do was hide, but where exactly was she meant to hide in a car?

The shadows whispered to her again, and for a second, Sarah shivered, only to realize they might offer her the answer. Hearing another noise, Sarah did the only thing she could think of. She scrambled into the driver's seat again, she unlocked the door, pushing it open as far as she could. It was barely enough to get an arm through, but hopefully, it would fool Joe for even a few minutes – time the cops and Veronica could use. Then she shifted carefully to the back of the car, down into the footwell, curling herself as small as she could. It wasn't easy to pull the blanket Joe had wrapped over her with her tied hands, but she managed it, turning her head to find a place to breathe. The shadows wrapped over her, pressing her down into the footwell and hiding her, she hoped, from immediate view. If Joe looked into the car window, he wouldn't see her immediately – but if he opened the door, her ruse was up. It was a dumb idea, probably something he'd be able to work out almost immediately, but it was the only thing she could think to do, the only thing that would give her a little more time.

"It's time for us to get reacquainted." Joe's singsong voice, suddenly higher pitched and different from anything she'd ever heard from him before, rang through the garage. Sarah squeezed her eyes closed, trying not to think about what he might do once he found her. "Not another word of a lie from you, now. From now on, we will be completely honest with each other."

Her ears straining, she heard Joe shoving back the filing cabinet, puffing as he moved it.

And then there was silence.

Footsteps broke through the stillness, and Sarah bit down hard, keeping herself as quiet as she could. Had he believed that, somehow, she'd escaped? There was nothing else she could do but to stay exactly where she was, no matter how uncomfortable she grew. All she was doing was buying time, praying that the cops or Veronica would find her before Joe worked out it had all been a ruse. Tears began streaming down her cheeks as she huddled there, feeling her arms and legs starting to numb from the unusual position.

Please come and find me, Veronica.

With a slight sniff, Sarah let the tears fall.

Please come and find me soon.

VERONICA

"She's not here. He took her."

Blood roared through her veins as Veronica ran back to Steve, Chase beside her.

"What?" Steve stared at her for a second before springing to life, albeit with the mask still attached. Pulling it from his face, he stared at Veronica. "I don't understand. Who? Why?" The EMT grabbed his arm and tried to get him to sit back down and put his mask on, but Steve shrugged the man off.

Chase wrapped one arm around her shoulders, pulling her tight against him, and she leaned into his strength, tired and overwhelmed with both shock and fear. "It was Joe."

Steve's face didn't register any sort of understanding. "Who's Joe?"

"Her mailman," Chase answered as Veronica took in a shaking breath, pushing back the tears that began to swell in her eyes. "We never even thought of him."

Steve took a step towards them. "Then we're going to get her, right?"

The EMT grabbed his arm and, this time, forced him to

sit back down. "What you're going to do is sit there and leave this on."

Steve shook his head. "I can't."

"You have to. And you'll have to go to the hospital to get checked over. I don't like the sound of the rasp in your chest."

Veronica moved closer to him, putting one hand on his shoulder as Steve groaned in frustration. "Sounds like you're not going anywhere. And neither are we, for the moment."

Steve's eyes flared. "Why not?"

"Because we can't just go running off." Turning, she held out one hand and Chase took it. "First thing to do is to tell the cops, and *then* we can think about the next step."

Chase nodded. "We need to be careful. It isn't something we can go into by ourselves."

"Right." Taking a beat, Veronica gestured to Steve. "I take it she never mentioned Joe?"

He shook his head no. "She's never said a word, but then again, talking about a mailman is one easy way to kill the vibe."

She nodded. "We need to think about where Joe might have taken her. My first instinct would be his place, but that's too obvious. He wouldn't go somewhere where he knew he could be easily found."

"But we don't know anything about him," Chase said softly. "How are we meant to find out where he's gone if we only have his first name?"

Veronica's gaze snapped to his. "Annie. She'll be able to help."

"Annie will be able to help with what?" Spinning around, Veronica pulled Annie into a bear hug that left her breathless. "I'm so glad to see you. You've come at the right time." Letting her friend go, she grasped her hands tightly. "I need you to find out everything you can about Joe."

Annie blinked. "The mailman?"

"Yes, Sarah's mentioned him sometimes, right? She said he was always really friendly and stopped to chat on her street now and again. He's the one who's got her, Annie. He's the one who's kidnapped our friend."

Annie's eyes widened for a few seconds, and she didn't say anything. She didn't even move, only to suddenly burst to life. "I'll go straight to the station." She still stumbled back, waving one hand in Veronica's direction. "I'll call you the second I find out anything. And you need to tell the police, Veronica. Tell them everything."

"Yes, I will." Spotting an officer climbing out of his car, Veronica walked to him directly.

"I'VE TOLD THEM EVERYTHING." Veronica threw up her hands and walked over to Chase, who quickly took her hand, obviously aware she was upset. "There's nothing else I could do."

"So what can we do?" Chase looked down at her, the confidence in his voice already building her up as Steve looked on. "I want to help."

"Thanks." With a sigh, she leaned into him. "I can't even think."

"Well, let's start from the beginning. You saw Joe take her, shoving her into the car but you don't think he'll take her back to his place."

She shook her head. "No, I don't think so. It would be the first place the cops would look, and he knows I saw him do it."

"Okay, so what next?"

In the following silence, Veronica closed her eyes, swinging away from Chase and trying to work through everything she knew about Joe so far. It was barely anything – he was a mailman and Sarah thought he was one of the friendliest guys around. It was likely most people thought the same. Would he go to his workplace? No, because then, no doubt, someone would see him. Had he taken Sarah out of town?

And what was he planning to do to her?

"Chase." Twisting towards him, she grabbed at his shirt. "You're in construction. I'm in real estate. Maybe we can work together."

Chase nodded, his eyes widening for a second as he realized what she meant. "Absolutely. I know a few guys I can call."

"What are you talking about?" Steve frowned, looking from one to the other.

"There's a chance Joe has another place somewhere." Speaking quickly, her thoughts flying around her head, she tried to order them one after the other. "He's been planning this whole thing – the fire, him grabbing her – was organized, so he's *got* to have somewhere prepared. I'm wondering if he's got another house nearby."

"Does it have to be nearby?" Steve asked as Veronica nodded slowly.

"I think it does. Whatever he pressed to her face, I don't think it would last all that long, not unless he was planning to give her another dose of something. I think he will stay close to home."

"There's one other thing." She tilted her head. "From what I remember, Joe has a dog."

"Does he?" Chase lifted his eyebrows as Steve scowled.

"A dog. Then he has to look after it, right?"

"I would hope so. I doubt he'd leave the dog alone for long – and he *definitely* didn't have it in the car with him."

Steve rubbed his chin. "So you think he might come back to get him?"

"Maybe." Pulling out her cell, she found Deborah's number. "Let me call Deborah. Hopefully, she'll be up for sitting outside Joe's house, just in case he comes back for his dog. The cops will be there soon, too, I hope."

"And what can I do?"

Veronica glanced at Steve, lifting the cell to her ear. "You need to go to the hospital. I'll call you if anything changes. Chase and I will head back to my office. There's a lot I need to go through."

Steve scowled, his jaw jutting forward, but he didn't argue, obviously aware that he wasn't in any fit state to go out searching for Sarah.

"We'll find her, Steve," she assured softly as the call to Deborah began to ring. "I promise."

A COUPLE OF HOURS LATER, Veronica was close to tears. "I was sure this would lead somewhere." Her head ached as Chase came to wrap her in a hug from behind, his arms going around her shoulders, his chin resting there gently. "If I'd realized this sooner, then Sarah might have been safe."

"This is not on you," Chase told her firmly. "You've done a great job so far. The cops are on it, too, remember."

"Yes, but they'll only be searching *his* place right now." Exhausted, Veronica stared at her computer screen. She'd drawn a blank, and Chase had too. He'd called a few friends, even though it was the early hours of the morning, but no one had come up with any new information about Joe and any potential houses he'd bought. "There's got to be something somewhere. We're just missing it."

Before Chase could say anything, Veronica's cell rang and she grabbed it quickly. "Annie? Any news?"

"Not much." Annie's voice was hoarse and Veronica wondered if she'd been crying. "The whole station is on this, Veronica, but they've come up empty so far apart from one thing."

"Which is?"

"Joe used to be married."

Veronica's eyebrows lifted, surprise wrapping around her chest as she put her cell on speaker so Chase could hear. "He used to be married?"

"Yep." Annie took in a small breath. "Her name was Sarah."

Veronica closed her eyes as her stomach rolled.

"I've only done a little digging — not officially, of course — but it seems like the marriage didn't end well."

Veronica grabbed a pen and jotted down the name. "Do you have a full name?"

"Her maiden name was Sarah Daniels. That's all I've got so far."

"And that's great." Finding Chase's hand, she clung to it, suddenly alive with energy. "We could do a search for her to see if there's any property in her name nearby."

"That would make sense. You probably have more real estate records than the police." Annie's voice shook. "If he's taken her to a place where he and his wife used to live together, then I'm worried about what that means for Sarah."

Closing her eyes tight, Veronica took in a deep breath. "I am, too, but let's hope it doesn't come to that. We're going to find her, Annie."

"I sure hope so," Annie whispered, her emotions obviously at a breaking point. "I'll stay here, see if I can find anything else out."

"Thank you." Ending the call, Veronica looked at Chase. "We need to search for a Sarah Daniels – any contracts or property in her name could change everything. Joe might still have access, or maybe he got it in the divorce – and that's where he's taken Sarah."

"Good thinking." With a grim smile, Chase picked up a

cell. "Let me make a few calls. They're going to hate me for waking them up again, but I'll explain it's an emergency."

For the next thirty minutes, she and Chase searched through every database they had access to and called every contact they had. Chase came up blank, shaking his head as he ended his twenty-third call as Veronica's desperation grew.

Then her gaze snagged on something.

"Wait, look there." She pressed one finger to the screen, heedless of the smudge it left behind. "There. It's a little place, but it's only a few miles out of town. It was bought about twenty years ago."

"You're right." Chase's hand was on her shoulder again, his voice lifting a little with anticipation. "Is there a chance she still lives there?"

Veronica shook her head. "I've been in this town long enough to know that Sarah would have heard about Joe's ex-wife if she still lived nearby. There's plenty of gossips in this town to talk about it." Pushing herself out of her chair, she turned to Chase, ready to hurry out to the car, only for Chase to wrap his arms around her.

"Take a breath, Veronica." Initially, she struggled, then let herself settle against him. When she did, he held her tight, her head on his shoulder. "We need to call the cops about this first."

"You're right." Lifting her chin, she looked up into his eyes, seeing the seriousness sitting heavily there. "So, how about this? I'll drive, and you make the call."

A few minutes later, they were out on the road. Veronica drove as fast as she dared, her heart in her throat as Chase spoke to the police, telling them what they'd discovered and where they were headed. She could hear the officer's voice coming through on the other end, telling Chase he needed to stay away, but Veronica saw him shake his head. Her heart swelled with love and admiration for the man who stuck by her no matter what happened. He was strong and stubborn and wasn't about to back down now.

"If we find anything else, I'll call you right back." Ending the call, he looked at her, his face masked by the shadows of the early morning gloom. "They weren't exactly pleased we were headed out there."

"There's nothing else I can do." Veronica shrugged her shoulders as Chase nodded firmly, gripping her hand for a second. "She's my friend. I have to find her."

"I get that." Letting out a breath, he nodded. "And I'm right here beside you."

They lapsed into silence as the road opened up. Veronica kept her eyes fixed, listening to the instructions of her app directing her where to go.

"This is the street." Chase squeezed her knee gently. "Maybe turn off those headlights."

Without a word, she did as he suggested. Dawn was already beginning to push forward, but Chase was right; it was best to be as cautious as they could. Moving slowly, she rolled the car slowly forward, the map telling her she still had a few yards to go. There were only one or two other houses, and from the looks of it, everyone was still in bed. There weren't any cars outside — in driveways or on the street — but maybe they were in the garage. Biting her lip until it was painful, Veronica jerked in surprise as the map declared that she'd reached her destination.

She kept driving.

"It's that one." Pointing at the house on her right, Veronica tried to get a good look at it. "That house right there."

Chase nodded. "It's the same as all those other houses. Just quiet."

"Okay. Let's get somewhere where we can see it, but if Joe

is there– we don't want him to notice us." Driving forward, she turned left and left again, down a small side street until she was parked directly in front of the house. A large tree concealed the streetlight, disguising them even more, and, turning off the engine, Veronica sat in breathless silence.

Everything in her body was tingling. Something told her that *this* was the place where Sarah was. Joe was here somewhere, too. She just couldn't prove it yet. "He's here. I know he is."

Chase didn't question her. Instead, he just sat beside her, his gaze fixed on the house. Silence flooded the car, but the nervous, tense silence had her heart pounding.

Without warning, the garage door was lifted and slid back. Before she could react, a man emerged, walking slowly out and looking from left to right, searching the street.

Veronica grasped Chase's arm. "That's Joe."

"What is he doing?" Chase's whisper matched her own as they watched Joe put his hands to his hips, turn around, and then, after a second, stride back to the garage. The door was pulled down and closed again, completely hiding him from view.

"She's there. We have to get to her."

Chase frowned. "You've got an idea, haven't you? We could just wait for the cops."

"Except we don't know what Joe might do to her in that time." Seeing him wince, she ignored the stab of fright, not letting herself think of the consequences of delaying. "So we have to take the lead."

"Okay." Chase squeezed her hand. "What's the plan?"

"First, we call the police. Second — Joe doesn't know you, does he?"

With a grimace, Chase glanced at her. "He doesn't. Why? Do you want me to go introduce myself?"

"Yep."

Chase's eyes widened. "Wait, what? You want me to go to his door and say hello?"

"I do." Nodding and ignoring the swell of anxiety that gripped her heart, Veronica gestured to the house. "He knows me from being at Sarah's during his delivery runs. He's been really careful about everything so far, so I'm sure he's already stalked all of Sarah's friends on social media. I'm worried he'd recognize me right now."

"Which is where I come in."

She nodded. "It's a risk, I know. I'll be there with you, just out of sight of the front door. You knock, and if – when – he answers, say you've been on a road trip and gone and got a nail stuck in the tire, and it's blown.... or our car is out of gas or something like that. Oh, and your cell phone hasn't got any juice left, either. You've been limping your way along for the last few hours until the car couldn't take it any longer, so now, you're looking for help."

It took Chase a second to agree. "Okay, I can do that. But – and this is serious, Veronica – what if he's got a gun?"

A tremor ran through her. "I'm guessing we run like hell."

"Helpful."

His ironic tone bit at her. "I don't think it's likely that he'll start shooting. He's trying not to draw attention to himself and keep himself and Sarah hidden. If he starts quizzing you about why you've come to *his* door, you could say that nobody else answered and, while you realize it's damn early, you didn't know where else to go. Play the sympathy card. You're cold and hungry, and you just need to borrow his cell. Maybe you could say something about seeing a light on?"

"Except there isn't a light on," Chase stated, only for a sudden gleam to flash from the top left window of the house. Veronica let out a breath of relief.

"I guess that's as good an excuse as any." With a wry smile, Chase laced his fingers through hers. "This is a big risk,

Veronica. Maybe you should stay in the car, and if the worst happens –"

"No." Interrupting him, she pressed his hand hard. "I'm coming. I'll hide out of the way, but I can't stay back here and watch you take the risk alone."

"The cops are coming."

She swallowed, tears catching in her throat. "I know, but every second she's in there is another second she's there with Joe. I can't leave her alone with him, even if the police *are* coming. We have to get her."

Veronica's chin lifted, her jaw tightened, and she pushed her tears back. "And we have to do it now."

SARAH

"You thought you could fool me."

Sarah winced, rearing back, her lip stinging as blood trickled down her chin. Sure, she'd bought herself a little more time when Joe had gone out looking for her, only for him to realize she'd been playing him for a fool. When he'd caught her, she'd been trying to get out of the car without him noticing since he'd moved the filing cabinet out of the way. But she hadn't managed in time. Her arm ached from where he'd dragged her from the car, her head spinning from the few blows he had delivered.

"Do you really think you can escape from me this time? I've got you again, and you're not going anywhere now. You and I are going to have our happy little life like we were always meant to." Joe's expression grew ugly. "You should never have left me, Sarah."

Struggling to contain the fear that began to spread cold through every part of her, Sarah turned her head away. Joe was talking to her as if she was someone else, but she didn't dare say she wasn't who he thought she was. She couldn't risk his reaction. He was angry enough already.

"You were going to leave me again, weren't you? That's why you were getting out of the car." Joe began to pace the bedroom floor as Sarah watched helplessly. After dragging her up the stairs, he'd pulled her into a large bedroom with a double bed, practically flinging her into an overstuffed chair in the corner. "You still think I'm not good enough for you?"

"Joe, I —"

"Don't speak." Screaming, he turned sharply, striding towards her, spittle flying from his lips. "You've already tried to explain, telling me I wasn't good enough for you, that I made your every day miserable. You have *no* idea what sort of man I am. I've worked hard on every single one of my flaws to try and get you back, and you *still* ignored me. Every letter I sent, every text message, every call – all nothing. You blocked my number, Sarah. I know you did, so this is what I've had to do to get my wife back." He flung his hands up and snorted as though she was the one responsible for what he had done before letting out another exclamation of what sounded like disgust.

Sarah kept herself as still as possible. Her breathing came in sharp gasps as tears streamed down her cheeks. Joe was caught in a delusion, and she didn't know what to say or do to get him to break free. The wrong word might push him to his limits. She might end up in an even worse situation than this.

"You're not going to have a choice this time, Sarah." Joe turned to face her. He was a dark silhouette against the dim light from the window. "You're going to stay here with me until you realize I'm the *only* man you need. None of those other guys are good enough for you." His hands dropped to his sides, his voice lowering. "You might have let me go once, but I'm going to make sure it doesn't happen again."

What could she say to that? Could she tell him that she wasn't the Sarah he thought? Try and break him free from his delusion somehow? Her mouth went dry as he strode across the room towards her. One hand grabbed her hair, yanking her head back as she cried out, but that only made him grin. Leering over her, he chuckled softly as Sarah closed her eyes, beginning to shake violently.

"You're going to stay with me, Sarah." Joe ran one finger down her cheek, and she let out a sob, unable to hide it from him any longer. "You're going to stay with me, and you're going to belong to me forever."

Even if she'd wanted to speak, terror stole all sense from her. The touch of his fingers on her skin drained her strength, and she slumped a little, her head still forced back.

"Look at me, Sarah." Joe's voice was low and dangerous, his eyes glittering when she finally met them. "Now, tell me how sorry you are. Tell me how you are sorry for breaking apart everything we had together, for making me feel like I wasn't good enough. Beg for my forgiveness, Sarah." A whisper floated towards her, and she closed her eyes again. "Beg."

She tried to speak, but the words wouldn't come. Her throat had clogged with fright, words stacking up, one on top of each other.

"Tell me, Sarah."

The whisper was gone now, anger rampaging through his voice instead. His hands went to her throat, closing around it, squeezing as he demanded she tell him what he wanted her to say. Then, he pressed with more force when she tried to speak. Laughing down into her wide eyes as she struggled to draw in air, the sound of her scream forced away by the pressure of his fingers. Her eyes widened, only to see darkness beginning to creep in at the edges. He was squeezing the life out of her, literally.

A sudden sound had Joe jerking back in surprise, his hands pulling away. Sarah took a huge breath before doubling over and coughing between gasps just as the sound came again.

Someone was knocking at the door.

"They can't have found me. Not yet." Joe hurried to the bedroom door and peered out into the hallway. The doorbell rang again, and Sarah closed her eyes, silently praying it *was* the cops. She had to escape or be rescued – if she didn't, chances were she wouldn't be leaving this place alive.

"Don't move." Joe spun around, coming towards her, grabbing at her shift, and half-hauling her out of her chair as he narrowed his eyes at her. "And don't make a sound. You know what will happen if you do."

After another second, he grunted and dropped her back down before striding out into the hall and pulling the door closed behind him.

Sarah stared at the door. He'd removed the handle from her side, which meant she couldn't get out, even if she managed to get her hands free.

Come on, Sarah. There's got to be something you can do.

Her wrists were rubbed raw from the cable tie, but she barely noticed the pain. Getting up, she walked to the window on shaky legs and peered through the grime, desperately hoping someone would see her.

There was no one there. No cop cars, nobody walking along the street towards the house.

Her heart sank.

So I'm still here alone. Tears began to flood her eyes, but she blinked them away, looking all around the room for something she could use to cut her hands free. Her whole body was weak and shaking, her vision a little blurred, and her energy gone, but at the same time, the desire to survive was strong.

I have to do this.

She could only find a rusty old nail sticking out of the

wall. It wasn't going to do much, but it was the only thing she could think of. Going to it, she slumped against the wall and began to scrape the cable tie over it again and again. It was painful and difficult and didn't seem to be making much difference, but gritting her teeth, Sarah carried on.

Wait, was that footsteps?

Joe was coming back.

Her heart screamed at her to hide. Using her last bit of energy, she rushed forward, flattening herself against the wall beside the door instead of going back to sit in her chair. She had one chance, one shot, to take him by surprise. She'd slam into him, then rush past to get out the door, to get *anywhere* other than here.

He might kill me.

Shuddering, Sarah closed her eyes and took in shaking breaths, feeling a little dizzy. There were sounds of other doors opening and closing, making her wonder if he'd forgotten where he'd stashed her. Had his delusions gotten so big he'd forgotten everything? She closed her eyes again, drawing in as much strength as she could, aware of just how tired she was. Slowly, the trembling lessened a little as she clasped her hands tight together, waiting for just the right moment.

The door opened... and Sarah jolted.

VERONICA

*S*omething heavy knocked into Veronica. Losing her balance completely, she fell backward just as the heavy weight crashed on top of her. Somebody was screaming, and she hit out, grasping at whatever or whoever was on top of her, afraid Joe had a partner to keep an eye on Sarah.

The screaming wasn't coming from this attacker, she realized as her hands tightened on the woman's shirt. It was coming from...*Sarah*.

Relief made her slump back on the floor, her hands loosening. "Sarah, it's me." Still keeping a hold of her friend, Veronica spoke loudly, trying to break through her friend's fear. "Sarah, you're safe. It's okay, it's *okay*."

It took Sarah a few seconds to realize it was Veronica and not Joe who had her, but eventually, Sarah slowly quieted and, after a few moments more, pushed away, bracing herself against the wall.

"You found me."

Sarah's voice was so subdued that Veronica's eyes flared, seeing just how exhausted her friend was. There were a couple of bruises to her face, her lip had split, and there was dried blood on her shirt. The redness about her eyes spoke of her suffering and fear. Veronica went to sit right beside her.

"Sorry it took so long. The cops are on their way."

Sarah, her body still trembling, dropped her head against Veronica's shoulder. "He thought I was someone else."

"Yes, his ex-wife," Veronica confirmed, speaking quietly. "She was also called Sarah. She left him a few years ago, and it seems like he never got over it."

"Where is Joe?" Sarah lifted her head suddenly, her eyes flaring wide. "Is he here? Is he coming back?"

"He's not going anywhere." A grim smile danced across Veronica's face. "Chase got him."

Veronica shared how she had crouched beside Chase at the front door, listening as she told the tale of getting lost and the blown tire, ready to beg for some directions and the use of a cell phone. That was when Veronica noticed the curtain twitching. Joe had glanced outside, then dropped it back into place, making no obvious move to open the door. Chase eyed the door and the surrounding frame, telling her in quietly that it would be easy enough to kick in. He hadn't waited for her to say yes or no but instead had kicked it once, then twice, and on the second time, the door had swung back so hard it had hit Joe square in the face. He'd been thrown back, almost knocked unconscious, and Chase had easily been able to restrain him. After that, Veronica had gone in search of Sarah.

"You're safe, Sarah." Shifting carefully, Veronica wrapped one arm around her friend's shoulders. "And I know one person is going to be absolutely thrilled to see you.

"Steve?"

"Yeah, Steve." She managed a small smile. "He was so mad when he had to go to the hospital instead of searching for you. He wanted to be looking for you."

Sarah lifted her head, her eyes still glossy with tears. "I'm looking forward to seeing him to," she murmured, before dropping her head back. "But right now, all I want to do is sleep."

Veronica smiled and nodded but didn't say anything else. Instead, she just held onto her friend tightly, waiting until the police came.

*****

"I THINK you've got a bit of a knack for this, Veronica."

Veronica managed a small smile but nothing more. She was bone weary after last night's events, which had stretched into the following morning. She didn't know how long she'd been awake for, but it had been a long time.

"So that's it. I think that's everything." It was the same cop who had dealt with her when there had been a vendetta against Chase, which was a little bit of a surprise. Picking up all of the sheets of paper, she put them in one folder. "Unless you have anything else to tell me?"

"I don't think I do." Rubbing one hand over her eyes, she shook her head. "I'm just glad Joe won't hurt Sarah – or anyone else – again."

"I can agree with you on that." The officer sighed. "Seems like Joe's been harboring an obsession with Sarah for years — ever since his wife left him and moved to another state, he's been secretly obsessed with her. It's almost as if he transferred his feelings for his wife to your friend." With a shrug, she sighed heavily. "I don't mind sharing this with you — we found a wall in his bedroom dedicated to Sarah. There were photos, newspaper cuttings, social media posts… anything that mentioned her name, he had it."

The information made her shudder. "And I never suspected him."

"Neither did we – but don't lose sight of the fact that you found her. You put the pieces together and worked out where she was. Like I said, you have a knack for this, and that gift has helped save your friend."

With a brief smile, Veronica let her gaze drop. Was this something she wanted to pursue? After all, she *had* started calling herself a private detective these last few weeks with the people she'd met. Was it something she ought to consider?

"I want to also thank you for keeping us in the loop." The cop shrugged. "Many of these detective types don't tell us anything, and that usually ends up going badly. I've appreciated that you've been calling us every step of the way." With a nod, she picked up her papers. "I think that's it. Unless you need anything from us?"

"What I need now is to go home and sleep." Veronica got up, pushing back her chair. "I don't remember the last time I felt so tired."

The cop smiled. "Then I hope you get some rest." She gestured at the door. "Oh, and if you ever do set yourself up as a private detective, please let us know."

"I will." Returning her smile, Veronica headed out of the station.

Stepping outside, she smiled as Chase pushed himself away from the wall and walked over to wrap her in his arms. She leaned heavily against him. "Are you okay?"

"I'm exhausted." Her eyes slid closed as she smiled. "But yes, I'm okay." Her head lifted, looking up at him. "Where's Sarah?"

"Still in there, I think. I imagine they'll be keeping her for a while."

Chase lifted an eyebrow as Veronica stepped back,

turning her head towards the door and immediately thinking she should wait for Sarah to come out. "And just in case you're considering staying, you don't need to wait. She's already got someone."

Veronica blinked at him. "She does?"

"Yeah, she does. Steve got discharged from the hospital about an hour ago, and this was the first place he went."

With a deep breath, Veronica closed her eyes again and leaned back against Chase, appreciating his solid strength. "I'm so glad to hear that."

"Then I guess we can go home."

Veronica didn't move, still leaning into him but tilting her head back to look up into his face. "Chase, how would you feel if I set up as a private detective?"

His eyebrows lifted. "You mean, give up real estate?"

Shaking her head, she stepped back just a little. "No, I mean doing it on the side."

Considering for a few seconds, Chase shrugged. "I think you'd be taking on a lot," he said honestly. "But I also think you're good at what you do. You could decide what cases you look at and which you don't. That way, you won't take on too much."

"Yeah, I could do that." With a deep breath, she wrapped one arm around his waist. "I have a lot of things to think about."

"And a lot of time to think about them," he reminded her quietly. "This isn't something you need to rush into."

"I know." With a grin, she tipped her head. "But if I ever *do* become a private detective, maybe I'll need a sidekick."

With a laugh, Chase pulled her close. "That sounds good to me."

SARAH

"*S*arah, I know you must be exhausted, and I'm sorry to have to keep you. I've only got a couple more questions."

Sarah nodded, grateful for the fresh cup of coffee she'd been given. "That's ok, I understand." The shock had begun to wear off at the hospital and even though they'd wanted to keep her in for observation, Sarah had refused and gotten herself discharged. Then, she'd been taken to the station and had been answering questions for the last hour or so. All she wanted to do was get this over with and get back home so she could crawl into bed.

"Do you know how long Joe has been obsessed with you?"

The question made her shiver, and she looked away. "I've had no idea."

"I'm sorry this is distressing." The woman pressed her hand briefly, although her gaze was steady. "We can take a break if you like?"

She shook her head. "No, it's okay."

The two cops exchanged a glance, with the man clearing

his throat and continuing. "In Joe's bedroom, we found an entire wall dedicated to you."

Her heart flipped over. "Dedicated to me?"

The woman nodded. "There were photographs of you going about your daily life – photos *he'd* taken. There were also printouts of social media posts, and any article where you or the firm you work at were mentioned, he'd posted up there. I'm guessing you had no idea about this?"

"None whatsoever." Nausea began to climb up her throat. "If I had known, I would have told someone about it."

"We understand." The man spoke gently, and Sarah took a breath, closing her eyes and reminding herself that they were just trying to establish the facts. "And he referred to you as Sarah, but you believe he didn't recognize you as yourself?"

"No." Again, she shuddered. "Joe thought I was his ex-wife. Veronica told me about her."

Again, the two cops looked at each other, with the woman clearing her throat gently. "Yes, Veronica has been doing a lot recently."

Sarah couldn't tell whether or not that was something they were pleased about.

"Joe's wife did leave him," the woman continued, gesturing to her files. "We discovered there had been an affair, and she had left him soon afterward to be with this other man. That obviously started the beginning of Joe's obsessive spiral."

"I had no idea." Sarah took in a steadying breath. "But I'm safe now, right?"

"Yes, absolutely." The man nodded reassuringly. "We have a lot of things to charge Joe with, the most serious being attempted murder." There was a momentary pause. "Do you think you'll be able to testify?"

"Absolutely." Courage had her lifting her chin. "I *will* testify."

"Thank you." He jotted something down on another bit of paper. "I don't think I have any more questions?" He looked to the woman, who also shook her head.

"I think that's it for the moment. I can see you're exhausted after everything you've been through. I'm sorry we had to do this immediately."

"It's okay. Thank you for all of your work." Sarah took another sip of her coffee and pushed herself up. "I appreciate it."

"You can thank your friend too." The woman smiled and shrugged at Sarah's questioning look. "She discovered more than we did, *and* she found you first. She's dedicated, for sure."

"Yes," Sarah agreed quietly. "She sure is."

Leaving her half-finished cup of coffee behind, she made her way to the front of the station. She only wanted to head home, curl up into a ball, and stay in her bed for however long it took to feel a little more normal.

"Can I call someone for you?" The man behind the reception desk looked at her. "Is there someone who can take you home?"

Sarah was about to ask him to call Veronica, only for a voice to break through the room first.

"I'm here for her."

Sarah turned just as Steve got up from his chair. She'd walked straight in, and, in her exhaustion, she hadn't even seen him.

"Steve." Her voice was a throaty whisper as she turned to him just as Steve opened his arms. Stepping into them, she leaned heavily against him, tears beginning to run down her cheeks. She didn't know how long they stood there, but Steve just held her close and as she cried, every single tear took some of her pain away.

"Let me take you home, Sarah." Steve looked down at her with eyes filled with concern. "Let me take care of you."

She couldn't say no. "Are you sure? After everything that's happened, you still want to —?"

"Of *course* I want to. I'm so glad you're safe." Ignoring the fact that they were in the middle of the police station, he dropped his head. "And just so you know, I'm already planning our next few dates."

Blinking through her tears, she wrapped her arms around his neck, letting him offer her the strength she needed. "I can't wait," she whispered. "Take me home, Steve."

"Sure." Dropping his head, he kissed her lightly before slinging one arm around her shoulders as they turned towards the door. Sarah stepped out with him, his strength holding her up. Her nightmare was over, and her bright future with Steve was only just beginning.

EPILOGUE

"*I*t's over."

Sarah closed her eyes and leaned into Steve's strong arms. The trial was over, the verdict had been handed down, and the dark, twisted memories began fading.

"It's over," she repeated, breathing Steve in as one hand rubbed her back gently. "And I'm home."

It had taken a long time for home to start feeling safe again. Even though Joe hadn't torched *her* place, she'd been jumpy and frightened for a long time. The knowledge of what he'd done, of how he'd watched her through her windows, hung around the streets outside, and left tulips at her door, had made her home feel like a trap.

How grateful she was for her friends and Steve. They'd understood and had helped her work through it. There had been the suggestion of moving – and Veronica had been more than willing to help with the sale – but in the end, she'd decided to stay. The more she'd thought about it, the more it felt like a victory for Joe if she'd given up the house she loved and moved somewhere else, and the last thing she'd wanted was for him to have any sort of triumph.

"Can I get you something? Coffee? Wine? Something to eat? I'm sure there's a ton of stuff in the refrigerator. And whatever you want for dinner, I can cook it or get takeaway. Whatever you want and whatever you need, okay?"

Sarah smiled and then lifted her head, looking up into Steve's face. His eyes were searching hers, his mouth tight, worry sending little creases into the corners of his eyes. He'd become more important to her than she'd ever imagined. Her fears about him turning tail and running once she'd told him about her stalker had faded away and been slowly replaced with a strength she knew would never leave her.

"I'm okay, Steve." Lifting her arms, she draped them around his neck and finally felt him relax, his shoulders dropping. "In fact, I'd say I'm more than okay. For the first time in a long time, I feel…free."

Steve took in a deep breath and smiled back at her. "That's because he's gone and won't be back for a long, *long* time…if he decides to return at all."

Sarah nodded, catching her lip between her teeth. It had been hard to testify and see him sitting there, watching her, but she'd found the strength to do it. Joe had been faced with a barrage of charges, including attempted murder, and he wouldn't be getting out any time soon – and even when he did, there would be restraining orders, probation officers, and all sorts of policies to make sure she was protected. She'd even had the chance to meet with Joe's ex-wife, the *other* Sarah, who had also testified about his behavior. What she'd disclosed to the court hadn't been pretty, and Sarah's heart had gone out to her. Little wonder she'd found someone else and left Joe behind. The guy had been terrifying.

"You don't need to think about it anymore." Steve let one finger run lightly down her cheek, smiling at her. "Yes, I know what you're thinking, but you can let it all go now. He's gone. It's done. You're free from it all."

"I couldn't have done it without you." Lacing her fingers behind his neck, Sarah closed her eyes for a second or two when he pushed his hand into her hair just as she liked. "I couldn't have done *any* of this without you – and without Veronica, Annie, and Deborah too. You mean so much to me, Steve. The way you've stuck by me and helped me through everything – helped me to cope! It's been incredible."

"I did it all because I love you."

The words came from him so simply, so quietly, but to Sarah, it was a roaring in her ears. Her breath caught in her throat, her eyes flaring wide for a second as she stared up at him, seeing his smile soften.

"Maybe this wasn't the right time to say it, but I couldn't wait any longer. I love you so much, Sarah. I love your strength, your courage, your determination. I love how you wake up with your hair all over the place and still look absolutely gorgeous. I love your kindness, the sweetness that just seems to bubble up from inside you. I love your loyalty and your fierceness when it comes to the people you care for. There's nothing I want to do more than be with you because the best place for me to be is right beside you."

Sarah's breath was rasping, tears burning in her eyes. For a second, she caught Steve's smile fading, his eyes rounding as if he was afraid he'd said the wrong thing, but then she pulled herself up on tiptoe and kissed him so hard her whole body exploded.

When they finally broke apart, both of them were gasping for air.

"I love you too, Steve."

Her words were ragged, but she stayed close to him, unable to bring herself to put even an inch between them. "I can't imagine what my life would be like without you in it. You've become everything to me, and I can't help but love you."

Steve let out a slow breath, then grinned at her. "Seems like something good came out of that dating app after all."

Laughing, she tightened her arms around his neck just a little, seeing the flash of heat in his eyes. "Something more than good, Steve," she murmured as his hands slid around her waist again. "Something incredible. Something amazing. Something I don't ever want to lose."

"That's good to know," he murmured, his head lowering. "Because I'm not going anywhere."

PARTY
SPARKS

A LAKE MINNETONKA COZY MYSTERY
LYSSA LUND

PARTY SPARKS

Next up in The Lake Minnetonka Cozy Mystery Series is Deborah's story in Party Sparks.

Deborah, a brilliant party planner, has always lived by one rule: never date a client. But when reserved accountant Thomas Granger hires her for a 40th birthday bash, sparks ignite beneath the surface. Their connection deepens after a magical first date, but when Thomas mysteriously disappears, Deborah is left with a cryptic note and a world of questions.

In "Party Sparks," love and mystery intertwine as Deborah unravels the truth about the man who captured her heart. Join her on a thrilling journey where the line between love and secrets blurs, challenging everything she thought she knew about trust, fate, and unexpected twists.

Get ready for a rollercoaster of emotions and a love story that transcends the ordinary. Will Deborah's heart lead her to the answers she seeks, or will Thomas Granger's secrets shatter her world forever?

Get Party Sparks Here

DEADLY DYNASTY

A MAYA RODGERS MYSTERY

TOP SECRET

LYSSA LUND

CHAPTER ONE

Stepping off the train onto the familiar platform of the station, Maya Rodgers pulled her briefcase behind her and sighed while she made her way through the congestion of commuters. She couldn't imagine ever taking the Metro Center Stations' architecture, with its curved ceilings and marvel of gargantuan escalators, for granted. The number of people who moved through here daily was an impressive feat of human engineering.

As she trudged down the busy Washington D.C. streets toward her Columbia Heights apartment, her mind was still reeling from the day she had just had. As a paid intern, she had been excited to work at the Washington Post, but today had been a frustrating experience. Though it wasn't what she had in mind all those years ago when she thrust herself into a journalism degree, being out here, making a life in D.C., she was proud of it.

Jeffery Arsenault, her editor, just gave her an assignment: secure an interview with a high-profile Virginia senator who was notoriously insulated and far too important, in her opinion, to give an interview to a lowly intern. Maya tried to explain the improbability, but Jeffery said, "I don't want you to tell me what's possible. I want results! This is your chance to prove yourself, Maya. This could pave the way to your promotion from an intern to a reporter. From fluff to substance. You have been here almost two years only because we have confidence in your potential. It's time to prove yourself." Maya was determined not to let this defeat her.

She had no idea how she would make the meeting happen, let alone get an appointment with Senator Wooley. A rumor afoot indicated he, among others in the Senate House, had been a part of an embezzlement operation based in Virginia. Something about fishing boat investments: Maya wasn't sure of the whole story but was crystal clear about Jeffery Arsenault's high expectations of her. Throwing a young intern into the sea without a life raft meant one thing; sink or swim. Maya considered herself a strong swimmer.

As she turned onto her street, she forced herself to push the thoughts of work out of her mind and focus on the task at hand, getting home. She made her way to the entrance of her building and stepped inside.

People in downtown D.C. were mostly decent, just not always friendly. In the time she had been living there, she had not made any close friends. People just didn't let you in. Most people were transient, and in her entire time living in DC, she had only met one native. In her experience, most people who came to DC stayed for a year or maybe two. Not long enough to put down roots. It was the work history for their resume they were after, not making long-lasting friendships.

Maya took her habitual trip by the mailboxes while fishing her keys out of her pocket. She rarely received mail anymore but couldn't stop the habit of checking. Today, something was behind the door of her small copper box. Maya opened the panel, pleasantly surprised someone would send her snail mail. With the same excitement as a child on Christmas, she dug her hand into the box, reaching for the thick, cream-colored envelope with her name on it.

Holding her curious treasure in her hand, she made her way through the hall, dodging the suspicious looks from Ms. Papayru from the eighth floor and a lengthy conversation with Mrs. Huffington on two. *Maybe one day I'll be able to afford a brownstone with a private entrance,* she mused as the ancient elevator brought her up to her floor and the humble apartment she had been so fortunate to find.

Once inside, she kicked off her boots and braced herself for the frigid confines of her studio. Accustomed to the quiet solitude of her life, and even though it was by design, Maya couldn't help but think back to how it used to be. Her childhood was not a kind one, but she remembered how she found it comforting knowing another soul was expecting her to come home. Flicking the light on, she took a deep breath and resolved to pay the expensive one-person electric bill first thing in the morning. Paying the bills from her meager income was challenging, but she somehow made it work.

Grabbing the Merlot off the counter, she flopped onto a tired velour loveseat and took a hefty swig of wine. Remembering her mysterious correspondence, she put the bottle down and grabbed it.

Opening the fancy linen envelope, she was surprised to learn it was a wedding invitation. Even more perplexing, it was from her best friend, Sandra Malone, whom she'd grown up with. They had sadly drifted apart since their first—and Sandra's last—semester of college.

Maya's heart started to race as she looked at the beautiful linen paper. Sandra's getting married! She couldn't believe it. They had been childhood best friends, and now Sandra had invited her to participate in the big day.

While the excitement swept her up momentarily, the

reality of Sandra's fiancé settled in with familiar nausea. Brandon Spencer was a demanding and possessive man. Even when they were all kids, Maya couldn't remember when they had not engaged in some battle over Sandra's attention. Yes, though Maya came from the other side of the tracks, so to speak, Sandra had never made her feel less then. Brandon, however, took every opportunity to let Maya know she didn't belong in their circle and that allowing her to hang around was more of a charity case.

The fact that she hadn't seen Sandra in the last two years was just another one of the ways Brandon had been successful in shutting Maya out of her life.

Maya eyed the invitation. She was happy for Sandra, but her face fell, thinking back to the abrupt way their long friendship had been cast aside and taken a back seat to Sandra's relationship with Brandon.

It seemed like they were kids just yesterday, and now Sandra was moving on to the next stage of her life.

Checking her phone and taking another bountiful swig of wine, Maya wrapped her dark curls into a messy bun. Understanding wine was not a food group, she peeled herself off the couch and cracked open the 1950s freezer. Just as quickly, she slammed the door shut and returned to the invitation she had just discarded to the overflowing coffee table.

Rereading the wedding details, Maya was invited to an all-inclusive Caribbean destination, all expenses paid, which was even more remote and exotic than she would have imagined. She pulled out the enclosed airline tickets. St Croix!

The flight was tomorrow!

It struck her as odd that she hadn't received a phone call, email, or warning from Sandy about this. Turning her full attention to the matter, Maya opened her computer, scrolled through her inbox, and searched her spam folder to see if she had missed some tip-off that a wedding was about to ensue.

She found the email. One month old. *How did I not see that?* she wondered as she clicked it open.

Dearest Maya,

It has been forever, it seems, since we've last spoken, I wanted to share some news with you. Brandon and I are getting married! It's all a bit spur of the moment, but we have decided to have a destination wedding! You will be the sole member of my bridal party. Lol. Your invitation, plane ticket, and itinerary are coming by mail (formally), but informally, I miss you! I hope you will be able to join us! Unless I hear differently from you, I plan to see you in St. Croix!

My Love,
Sandy

Maya understood that Sandra must be excited about the wedding, but it had seemed strange that she wouldn't have at least given her a heads-up. Maya breathed a sigh of relief that she wasn't an afterthought and that her lack of response would not be considered a faux pas, but trepidations about spending a week secluded with Sandra's future in-laws made a chill run down her spine. *This was going to be interesting*, she thought.

Realizing she would have to figure out how to approach her boss to take time off of work and then get organized to leave the next day, Maya imagined Jeffery's denial at the other end of a call she had yet to make. With a sigh, she slumped down on her couch again, staring at the invitation, trying to absorb it all.

* * *

Walking through the terminal, Maya considered the unusual windfall. She had never had a trip paid for by someone else. The family Sandra was marrying into had money to spare;

however, it wouldn't have been a cavalier donation for the likes of *her*. The Spencers hadn't rolled out the red carpet for her before, and she would never have been able to afford this trip on her own, so a big thank you would be in order no matter how difficult it would be to be looked down upon by the Spencer family again.

After arriving at the airport, Maya's head spun from the past few hours—a whirlwind of preparations and excitement. She hadn't slept.

Realizing she still needed to call her office and have the dreaded conversation, she pulled her phone out of her purse. Dialing the number and preparing for the onslaught, Jeffery picked up the second ring, "Maya, where are you?" he barked.

"I'm at the airport, sir. I wanted to give you a heads-up. I won't be able to come in today," she said, trying to sound sure of herself.

Silent for a moment, Jeffery finally said, "Maya, do you realize you have a challenging assignment to start, and if you're not here in 15 minutes, you can find a new internship?"

A red-hot wave washed over her. Swallowing down the fury that would burn this bridge while standing on it, she closed her eyes and told herself a quick lie," *I am confident; I have a lead for this story; he needs to trust me.*"

Maya covered every fluff story for the past two years at the Post. She had never missed a day and endured all the humiliation thrown at her. Jeffery only gave her this goose chase in this one instance to see if it would break her. That much she was sure of.

She would never have thought twice about prioritizing her position over her best friend in another lifetime, but that was before real-life kicked in. Now, as she sat on the plane, a ball of nerves, she had to find a way to blend both aspects of her life. What better way to do so than to dig around with high society?

"Sir, I am heading to a venue in the Caribbean for a wedding. In fact—" *take deep breaths, you can do this,* she thought, noticing her hands were clamming up, "—while yes, a personal element is involved, the guests attending are all a part of the most wealthy and influential circles in Virginia, sir.

"It all sounds terribly convenient, Maya." He said.

"It is the wedding of the son of the Spencer family, a close childhood friend of mine. I have researched the guest list, and at least a handful of these attending are connected to and may have a thing or two to say about Senator Wolley. I have been invited as a member of the bridal party. It will allow me to get close to everyone. Both the bride and groom will help me get connected."

"If that is true, it is a lucky opportunity. I expect you to work the crowd, Maya. I need you to check in regularly and update me on your progress. Understood?"

"Yes sir, thank you, sir!"

Hearing the change in Jeffery's tone, Maya couldn't believe she had gotten his approval. How she would wrangle interviews and pursue leads while trying to be in a wedding was beyond her, but she'd find a way. That's what friends were for.

* * *

"Sandy?" Standing outside her friend's hotel room, Maya dabbed at the sweat beads beginning to form on her brow. It was 11:30 a.m., and the hundred guests for this marriage were all packed under the white tent, waiting in equal parts anticipation for a glimpse of the bride and relief from the heat.

Maya hadn't been invited to any pre-wedding festivities, including helping Sandra prepare the morning of the nuptials. While Maya had never been a part of a wedding party before, it struck her as strange, but she assumed all was handled by Sandra's Mother-in-law, Miranda. Miranda had been instrumental in raising her soon-to-be daughter-in-law. After Sandra's parents died, Miranda did the school runs, the bake sales, and the birthday parties. Though Sandra was marrying her son, over the years, a bond grew so strong between them that she was who Sandra considered her mother figure.

Maya's itinerary said to meet at the chapel at 11:00, ready to go. Still, when Sandra hadn't shown up by 11:15, and no one seemed concerned, Maya took it upon herself to check on what was keeping Sandra and accompany her in case she had pre-wedding jitters and needed some moral support.

"Sandy! It's 11:30! Everyone is waiting! Are you okay?"

Maya's jiggled the door handle, surprised at the ease with which it opened. The flowery curtains were still drawn as if the morning sun touched every inch of this Caribbean paradise except the bride's quarters.

"Sandy," she whispered, hoping with every fiber of her being that there was a reasonable explanation she was late. Maybe she had just missed her friend. Maybe Sandy was already at the beach. Perhaps the maid left the door open.

Maya approached the bed, finding it odd that Sandra had not even opened the curtains or patio glass doors. Peering into the shadows with trepidation in her heart, Maya barely made out the silhouette of her best friend's motionless body. Maya stepped closer, following the vague outline of the bed until she faced the now lifeless figure of her closest child-hood friend, still in her pajamas. Eyes still open, Sandra lay staring into the blank realm of death, a death which came in many colors but always ended the same. Backing away in stunned silence, Maya lost her footing. Stumbling backward, she hit the adjacent wall, slumping down until she crouched eye-to-eye with Sandra's empty face. As if then, it became somehow more apparent than a moment ago; the reality crashed into her as a wave of destruction, questions, and heartbreak. She let out a scream.

Miranda Spencer, a handsome mid-50s woman, was not the type of mother to tolerate social discrepancies. Approaching her daughter-in-law's hotel room, she heard a scream from the elevator entrance. Noticing it came from the direction of Sandra's room, she jogged from the elevator, giving herself time to work out what could be going wrong. Quickening her stride, Miranda stopped short in the hall outside the door. Finding the door ajar, she yelled, "Sandraaa! Sandra!" with every ounce of venom a woman of her stately stature could conjure.

Stepping into the dark room, she felt fearful tears creep up behind her eyes. "Sandra, answer me!"

Cruel understanding dawned at the sight before her. Falling on her knees, Miranda let out a guttural cry, a scream so deep, so devastating, that it resounded through the hallways and out to the ocean.

The pain at seeing the lifeless Sandra was too much to bear.

* * *

The mood was somber in the privacy of the lounge. The hotel reserved the area for the immediate family and wedding party following the news of the bride's death. Money was not a concern for those guests awaiting the day's event, so most left the resort for other accommodations, glad to be free of the quarantine grief of the family.

As Maya sipped her whiskey, she mulled over the events

of the previous 24 hours. Nothing about this made sense, and they could not identify what or who caused Sandra's death until the investigation was over.

For Maya, the question of who might have done this couldn't be shaken. In many instances, both fantastic and mundane, feelings clouded judgment. But in the case of Maya, her intuition screamed that something was wrong. This death was no accident.

Swishing the ice cube around in her glass and looking out the window at the sun beginning its descent, she finally returned to her senses, wondering how long she had been lost in her thoughts.

As if Brandon, "the groom that was not to be," read her mind, their eyes locked. Brandon had never liked Maya. The idea of Sandra having relationships outside of theirs was inconceivable within the Spencer household. Telling a Spencer 'No' wasn't accepted with that sort of old money.

What was it, Sandy? What did you say no to this time?

Brandon Spencer grew up in a world that had carved out a separate reality for him. While they were kids, and until all three of them were heading off to college, Brandon had always gotten everything he wanted.

Brandon had been seething with anger at the prospect of Sandra attending the same school as Maya. She was not following him to his Ivy League School on a ticket she hadn't earned. Maya remembered that morning. As they packed to leave, Brandon showed up banging on the door. Over the years, Maya learned to avoid him during those tantrum-fueled episodes. This time for Sandra's sake, she stayed to help share the burden.

"I can't believe you would go through with this!" he screamed in her face, kicking boxes and smashing whatever was accessible.

"Please, Brandon, stop! We will still be together. Nothing

will change that. I just need a change of pace!" Sandra pleaded, all the time shielding herself behind the couch.

Without warning, he rushed her, grabbing her by the arms, "You will regret this if you leave me, Sandra. Do you understand me?"

They left for school the next day with Sandra wearing a black eye.

See Deadly Dynasty here

FREEBIE

As a Thank you for reading my book, I'd love to offer you another title for free.

A Touch Of Prophesy

You are invited to download this book as my gift here. Or you can get it @ www.lyssalund.com

THANK YOU!

Thank you for reading my books! I know you have so many choices and I am honored you have chosen to read mine.

As an independent author I really depend on your reviews to help new readers take a chance on my work. If you enjoy Petals Of Peril it will help so much if you can take a few minutes to leave a review.

Amazon is preferred if it is possible for you to do so. Goodreads and Bookbub are helpful too.

Happy reading!

xoxo, Lyssa

ABOUT LYSSA LUND

About Lyssa Lund

Lyssa Lund discovered her love of reading in first grade when she discovered Hans Christian Anderson and The Brothers Grimm fairy tales.

Lyssa is an avid reader and writer who understands wanting to escape and be carried away by the story. While keeping it clean, Lyssa aims for the best in strong female characters, heart-of-gold alpha heroes, mystery, suspense, and heartwarming romance.

Lyssa lives in the upper midwest, where the winters are long and cold and perfect for reading and writing by the fire. She shares a home with her wonderful husband Craig, and Borzoi hound, Isa.

She adores reader feedback at hello@lyssaLund.com.

Find out more about Lyssa at lyssalund.com

ALSO BY LYSSA LUND

Shadows Of Dark And Light

A Touch Of Prophesy

The Dark King's Heart

The Sylvan Wilds

Witches Will Rise - coming soon

The Borderland Guardians

The Blizzard Crossing

Beyond Aorel

The Hall Of Divinity

Realms Of Destiny Series

The Lost Heir Of Isla

Kingpin Of Topree

Maya Rodgers Mysteries

Deadly Dynasty

Ink and Blood

Brushed By Danger

Sleight Hand Of Death

Lake Minnetonka Cozy Mysteries

Secrets Buried

Petals Of Peril

Party Sparks

Silver Mist Cove Cozy Mystery Series

The Witches Inheritance

The Mother's Legacy

The Faerie's Vow